I wish my job as a magical librarian was just about shuffling books and shushing people from behind a desk. Alas, the magic I wrangle requires a bit more than shuffling and shushing. And to make things worse, I have a frog and a cat, and I have no idea how to use them!

Sure, I understand, we all have bills to pay. Personally, I could use a bit of extra cash too. But I'm pretty sure I wouldn't kill for it. At least...not without dark magic influence. And that's exactly the problem.

Dark. Magic. Influence.

My first challenge for the day is finding that artifact and putting it under lock and key before it kills anybody else.

My second challenge is figuring out how to deal with a bossy frog and a pushy cat.

Which of the two do you suppose will give me the bigger headache?

Yeah. That's what I think too. The frog and cat are going to be the death of my sanity.

Maybe I should put them under lock and key too.

FORTUNE CROAKIES

SAM CHEEVER

ELECTRIC PROSE PUBLICATIONS

APPLE TREES AND FROG PEE

*I*t isn't every day that you find yourself staring at a frog's squishy butt bulging from the underside of a sink drain. I would have felt better if I'd believed it would never happen again. However, because I appeared to be frog-cursed, there was a strong possibility I'd eventually end up lying on my back under the sink, eyeing the posterior region of Mr. Slimy again.

Sighing, I gave the squishy bulk a tentative poke with my finger, earning a forlorn, "Ribbit!" for my efforts. Something trickled downward, hitting my cheek and dripping down to the paper towel I had draped under my head to keep "under the sink" cooties off my hair.

I realized, too late, what had just dripped on me.

"Argh!" I shoved out from under the sink and bent over while grabbing frantically for more paper towel to wipe frog pee off my cheek. "I can't believe it!"

The figure lounging against my refrigerator grinned. "You shouldn't poke a stressed frog, Naida."

I glared at the source of almost all my problems.

Okay, I know I previously said that about Mr. Wicked, my adorable kitten who was probably better at being an artifact keeper than I was. But I'd reassessed the players and decided Rustin Quilleran, former witch and current frog squatter, was definitely more trouble than my sweet little kitten.

I mean, Wicked was curled up on his pillow, purring happily.

Rustin was driving a fat frog bus that got itself jammed in my drain and peed on my face.

I'll let you do the math.

"Not funny. You need to keep a better lock on the contents of your bladder."

His grin widened. "I think you have a mistaken view of my ability to control your wedged friend," he told me. "I'm just a passenger on that particular bus."

Which, normally I'd be happy about. I mean, when Rustin had gotten stuck in the frog because of a spell his horrible family had performed, I'd felt terrible. We'd tried everything to get him out of there. But, in the end, the evil Jacob Quilleran had interfered, making certain poor Rustin didn't escape the fate Jacob had locked him into.

I still hadn't found out why Rustin's Uncle Jacob had felt the need to lock him in a frog.

Rustin wasn't being very forthcoming with the information.

I hurried past him, into my bathroom, where I put soap onto the wet paper towel and scrubbed my cheek until I was in danger of removing a layer of skin cells along with the frog pee.

"What are you doing here, then? Standing there laughing isn't helping at all."

Rustin shrugged. "I was bored. Your life is generally good for a few laughs. I'm happy to report that this morning has been no exception."

I barely resisted zapping him with my almost worthless keeper magics. I pretty much had only enough oomph in my zapper to curl someone's hair or make them pee themselves.

Trust me when I tell you I'd had enough of making stuff pee for the day.

Flinging the soiled paper towel into the trash, I glared at him. "I'm so glad I could entertain."

"Me too." His grin never wavered.

A part of me was happy to see it. I'd been so worried that Rustin would lose his humanity because of his enforced incarceration in the frog. But his cousin Maude and his very powerful Aunt Madeline had been working on reversing the spell. They hadn't managed yet to free him. But they'd created a metaphysical barrier between Mr. Slimy's — a.k.a.

the frog's — consciousness and Rustin's so he could maintain his power, brain capacity, and humanity... basically his soul.

That was as good a result as we could have hoped for under the circumstances.

Even though that meant, as Mr. Slimy's current foster parent, I was also the unlucky owner of the ethereally handsome and eternally snarky witch who was stuck inside the frog.

You thought I was kidding about the challenges of my life, didn't you?

The bell jangled downstairs in my bookstore, and I glanced at my stuck amphibian.

"Ribbit." Slimy's sticky tongue snapped out and snagged a massive fly that had tried to make a break for the window above the sink.

Sucker.

I looked at Rustin. "Keep an eye on the squishy, green bus. I have to go see who's downstairs."

He nodded, casting what appeared to be an affectionate glance toward Mr. Slimy.

I shook my head. How anybody could be fond of a frog was beyond me.

Although, I realized as I bounced down the steps to the first floor, that I'd begun to form an attachment which transcended disgust. In fact, I almost dreaded the day Madeline managed to find a way to extract her nephew. I was going to miss him.

Unlocking the door that separated the bookstore

from the artifact library behind me, I blinked in surprise.

Had I just had a Freudian moment? Was I going to miss the witch? Or the frog?

I shrugged, shoving the question aside for another time. It would probably be an easy choice.

I mean, one of them just peed on me.

My friend Lea was standing in front of the bookstore entrance with something large and red balanced on her hands. She was holding it out in front of her like an offering, a wide smile on her pretty round face. "We have apples!"

A small, gray kitten with dark gold eyes bounced in behind her, tail waving lazily on the air. Lea's new kitten, Hex shot past me and through the cracked door into the artifact library, no doubt looking for my cat Mr. Wicked.

My mouth fell open. "That's an apple? I thought it was a giant ball or something."

I wandered toward her, my gaze locked on the enormous, shiny fruit.

She was just about dancing with excitement. "Fairies!" she squealed happily.

Lea ran the herbalist shop next door, and she had a giant greenhouse out behind her shop. The greenhouse had recently had a large influx of Fae when the Quilleran clan had burned their homes in the Enchanted Forest...long story...to the ground.

Everyone knows that one of the side benefits of

having Fairies was that, if you're on good terms with them, they blessed your garden. What I'm not sure many people understood, including me, was exactly *how* blessed it could become.

I lifted an awed look to Lea's overjoyed face. "I didn't even know you had apple trees."

"I didn't," she exclaimed happily. "Until a couple of weeks ago. They're already five feet tall." She gave in and did the little happy dance she'd been trying not to perform. "I can't believe these apples. And you should taste them. Sweet, crisp and perfect." She rolled the apple around on top of her hand so I could see its perfect skin.

"That's amazing!" I agreed, laughing. "And I'm more than a little jealous right now."

Her expression softened. "This is actually for you. Queen Sindra insisted. I'm to provide as many of these and the peaches she's currently nurturing as you'd like. To thank you for saving her daughter."

I took the apple she handed me and barely kept from doing a little happy dance of my own. "Sweet Caroline," I said, licking my lips.

The front door opened again and a strange-looking creature with fire-red hair, a pale face covered in freckles, and large pointed ears stepped into my shop.

I would have expelled her immediately if I could have. Not because she was dangerous. But because she looked even crankier than usual and I was on an apple high. I didn't want her to bring me down.

Lea turned to my city Sprite and gave her an impulsive hug. "Good morning, Sebille."

Sebille narrowed her iridescent green gaze suspiciously. "Have you been licking your frog again?"

Lea giggled. "Wally doesn't have any psychedelic grease. He's a bullfrog."

Sebille rolled her eyes, a fairly regular habit with her. "Stop smiling you two, it's annoying." She shuffled over to the counter to plunk her enormous, ugly bag on the shelf beneath.

We eyeballed her strange garb, which currently included black, red and white striped socks that started somewhere under her skirt and ended in shiny red "wicked witch of the west" shoes. Her dress was dark green, with tight sleeves that hooked over each of her thumbs, and tiny yellow and white flowers embroidered all over it.

She'd plaited her long hair into two braids that separated around her oversized ears.

I decided to take the bull by the...erm...braids. What can I tell you? Once you've been peed on by a frog, you really have nothing left to lose. "What's got your granny panties in a twist today?" I asked my assistant.

She glared through the bangs she'd been recently growing out. They hung into her eyes more often than not and gave her a bad-tempered imp look. "I'm being evicted."

Lea and I shared a horrified look, probably both thinking the same thing.

What if she wants to move in with one of us?

Lea poked my arm and I shook my head. "Nope, not happening. I'm already babysitting a smart-mouthed witch ghost and a frog that jams himself into the sink drain and then pees on my face."

Lea frowned, seemingly trying to untangle the imagery I'd just spewed in her direction, then shook her head. "I've got you beat. I have five...maybe seven..." She cocked her head. "I keep losing count. I have hundreds of Fae in my garden. I'm Fae'd out."

A forceful sigh yanked our attention back toward Evicta the Homeless Sprite. "You're both heartless shrews."

Lea shrugged and I nodded. If keeping my space grouchy-Sprite-free made me a shrew, then I'd happily wear the badge.

"Why'd you get evicted?" I asked Sebille, walking over to place my head-sized apple on the counter. I needed to take it upstairs where I could happily hoard it until it was totally consumed. But I needed to make sure Sebille's search for a new home took her in the right direction.

Namely, any direction but mine.

She gave the apple a cursory look, no doubt used to giant apples since she was a Sprite. "I might have over-vaped and turned one of Devard's best customers...temporarily...into a slug."

Devard was the owner of the vapery across the street.

When Sebille saw the horror on our faces, she held up her hands. "Just for a blip. The guy hardly even had time to slime a path to the door before he was back again. Besides, he didn't even know he was a slug until that stupid woman with the frizzy hair started screaming like a Banshee."

I frowned. "You mean the Banshee who lives across the street?"

"Yeah," Sebille agreed, warming to her complaints. "What's with all that screaming anyway? Don't those weirdos have anything better to do?"

Lea and I shared a look.

Sebille had taken an apartment over the vapery, and she spent most of her free time creating and then sucking special vapes made with...unique... herbs. She was known, on occasion, to share her special concoctions with others. Those occasions were generally problematic.

I'm pretty sure I'd climbed the fire escape on the side of the building the one time I'd tried Sebille's special vape. There are rumors that I'd tried to ride a large crow, insisting it was my own personal dragon.

Shredded-crow-psyche aside, I'd almost died that night.

Yeah. You heard that right. I just made it about me.

That crow should have known better than to stick around when I hit the roof. He should have seen the madness in my eyes and disembarked toot suite! The fact that he hung around, cawing at me as if he were laughing at my attempts to saddle him, made him just as much to blame for what happened as I was.

And no, I didn't hurt the crow. Except for his pride.

I'm pretty sure those feathers on his head will grow back.

Lea suddenly decided she had to go. "Um...I'll see you ladies later."

"What about Hex?" I asked my quickly retreating friend.

"I'll come back for her in a couple of hours."

The door was slamming shut behind Lea as my gaze found Sebille's. "It shouldn't be hard to find another place," I told my assistant.

She shrugged. "Not one I can afford. My place is really cheap." She gave me a slightly hostile look, as if the salary I was paying her was part of the conspiracy to see her homeless.

I bit back a defensive retort and patted her on the shoulder. "We'll find you a great place. But right now, I have something I need to do upstairs." I grabbed my apple and headed toward the stairs.

"Naida?"

I stopped in the doorway. "Yes?"

She fidgeted with the stapler and calculator, her gaze avoiding mine. "Do you think I could sleep here just until I find a place?"

My heart broke a little at the sight of her. She was so embarrassed to ask. And despite my cocky response to the news that she'd been evicted, I knew I couldn't let her hit the streets.

I swallowed the enormous lump in my throat and nodded. "Sure. But maybe it won't come to that. There have to be a ton of cute studio apartments in Enchanted."

She grimaced, nodding. "Thanks."

I spun on my heel and made my way back up the stairs, my step a lot heavier than it had been before. Lifting my chin, I squared my shoulders. I'd find Sebille a place to live if it was the last thing I did.

But, in the meantime, Sebille's earlier snarky comment to Lea had inspired me.

And I had a frog to grease.

2

MOVING AND OTHER HORRORS

*T*he day started off badly. I'd thought I'd have a few days to prepare mentally for having Sebille move into Croakies, but, alas, her narrow butt walked into the bookstore the very next day with a box so big it obscured her from the waist up.

She struggled coming through the door, and I jumped up from the tall stool behind the counter and hurried over to hold it for her. "Oh my!" I said, eyeing the enormous box. "Why didn't you magic it down to a more manageable size?" I whispered my question because Mrs. Foxladle was in the cozy mystery aisle, perusing the new additions with the discerning eye of a true connoisseur.

As far as I knew, the octogenarian didn't have a magical bone in her upright, nimble body.

An iridescent green eye and half of a fiery red

head appeared around the side of the box, fixing me with half of the disgust Sebille usually showed me.

But only because the other half was currently hidden behind the box.

"I did magic it, Naida," she whispered harshly. "How else did you think I got all my furniture inside?"

My mouth fell open, and all the spit immediately dried up. This thing...this horror from my most terrifying nightmares...Sebille moving into my beloved private zone...was actually happening.

"I..." I swallowed hard, but since my mouth was dry, it just choked me, sending me into a coughing fit that earned me another dose of one-eyed disgust from the city Sprite.

"Where do you want me to put this?" she asked in normal voice.

I bit back my knee-jerk response, which went something along the lines of, *In another solar system, far, far away*. Opting instead for, "In the back, I guess."

Nodding, she struggled toward the dividing door between the bookstore and the artifact library. I hurried ahead to grab the door for her, smiling as Mrs. Foxladle came around the end of the mystery aisle with an armful of paperbacks. "Did you find what you wanted?" I asked, closing the door firmly behind Sebille.

Mrs. Foxladle gave me a smile, her gray eyes

bright with excitement. "Oh, yes! Thank you for letting me know the new Samantha Delingpole book was here. I've been waiting so long for it to come in!"

I smiled back, her excitement infectious. "I'm so glad I could get it for you. I've already had several other requests for the book. I thought I might have to hide a copy under the counter for you."

She chuckled. "That's probably my book club. I waited to tell them about it until I knew you had several copies." She flushed guiltily. "I love them, but not that much."

I laughed with her. "Let's get you checked out."

I rang up the three cozies, all featuring beautiful cats and cute titles, and put them into a small paper bag with handles. The bags were emblazoned with the name, Croakies, and had a picture of a big-eyed frog squatting on a leather-bound book that looked a lot like my favorite artifact. The Book of Pages.

I'd discovered the book several weeks earlier in the search for a particularly elusive artifact, and had been experimenting with ways to make use of it. It turned out the Book of Pages was a keeper of the artifacts tool that I hadn't known about.

It had made my job a lot easier to do.

Handing Mrs. Foxladle the bag, I told her, "I added a couple of my new bookmarks to the bag. I think you'll like them." I'd created the bookmarks from a picture of my beautiful kitten, Mr. Wicked and my newest foster child, Mr. Slimy.

So far they'd been very popular.

She glanced inside, seeing the three bookmarks I'd dropped on top of the books, and exclaimed. "Oh, is that your beautiful fur-baby?"

"Mr. Wicked, yes. And...a friend."

Her eyes sparkled with pleasure. "I love them!" She patted my hand. "I hope you bought a lot of them, hon. Because I'm going to show them to all my friends and they'll probably flood the place to get one."

"I'm ready," I told her, squeezing her soft, warm hand. "Thank you so much for your business."

I watched the elderly woman stride briskly from the store, feeling good. The bookmarks had been Lea's idea. She'd noticed how popular Mr. Wicked was with customers and thought it would be a good reminder to everyone who visited the store once that they'd probably enjoy a return visit.

So far, they seemed to be a huge hit.

The bell jangled behind Mrs. Foxladle, and I heard her speaking to someone outside the door. I looked up from the pile of orders I was sorting and saw a face I remembered but couldn't quite place.

The woman was beautiful, magically so, with bright blonde hair and eyes the color of a sun-drenched Caribbean ocean. She held the door for Mrs. Foxladle, earning my respect and the smile that came to my face. "Good morning," I said as she approached me.

"Hi, Naida."

I blinked, fighting to remember the face. She must have read the struggle in my expression because she waved a hand over her face, turning her hair dull and her features soft, the eyes haunted and the lips settled into a perennial downward curve.

The memory clicked into place. "Alissia Gibbon!"

She nodded, letting the glamour slide away. "Sorry about that. I sometimes forget when people meet me outside the shop they don't recognize me."

Alissia had shown me her true self when we'd been there setting a trap for a local witch family that was up to no good. But I'd only seen it for a few seconds. The memory of her glamoured visage was set deep into my memory.

Alissia owned *Mythic Specialty Teas* on the other end of Enchanted. She was a sorceress like me. Also, like me, her magical abilities were limited mostly to her legacy magic, which, in her case was dealing with magical herbs and teas.

"It's so nice to see you again," I told her, giving her an impulsive hug. "I never got a chance to thank you for what you did...helping us take down the Quillerans."

She shook her head. "It was what needed to be done. I'm just glad we managed to stop them."

I nodded. "What can I do for you today? Are you looking for a book?" My eyes widened. "Oh, I just got a great volume on teas to ward off failure and mistakes. It was an obscure enough topic, I thought of you."

She nodded. "Yes, I'd definitely be interested. I haven't studied that area overly much." She glanced quickly around the shop, leaning close. "Are we alone?" she whispered.

"Yes. My assistant's here, but she's in the back."

"Good." Alissia seemed to relax. "I have a problem I was hoping you could help me with."

"Of course. What is it?"

"I think the restaurant next door has gotten hold of an artifact."

I nodded. "Did they steal it or otherwise get it illegally?"

"I believe it was recently passed down to him by a family member."

"Has he misused it? Harmed others with it?"

She looked frustrated. "None of that, no. I just..." Alissia frowned. "He's just not himself. I can't explain it. But I think the artifact is doing something to him."

"Like what?"

"He's always been such a kind man. Generous to a fault. He gives unsold food to the poor in the area and lets first responders eat at a deeply discounted price." She smiled. "He even feeds the strays that show up in the alley. He and his wife are just the sweetest young couple."

"And that behavior has changed?"

"*She's* still the same," Alissia hurried to assure me. "But the husband..." she shook her head. "He snapped at a man asking for help yesterday, telling him to get away from his restaurant. And I witnessed him chasing a couple of stray cats away from the back door." She frowned. "I was in there for lunch the other day. His face was... I don't know how to describe it."

"Haggard?" It was the best term for what I'd seen so many times. Part of my job as keeper of the artifacts is to counsel people on the use and care of them. Unfortunately, when a family passes an artifact down, they don't always take the time to explain how to use it safely.

"I don't get involved unless an artifact has been acquired illegally. Or if it's being abused in some way," I told her.

Judging by the lines between her eyes, Alissia was unhappy with my response. I didn't blame her. "But, I do sometimes help people cope with artifacts. Maybe I could talk to them."

The frown slid away from her face. "Oh, would you? I'd appreciate that. I'm really worried about them."

I stared at her for a long moment, wondering about the source of her concern. The things she described to me were unfortunate, but hardly enough to make a virtual stranger lose sleep. I had to wonder what was really going on. "I generally perform the service at the request of the artifact owner. But your neighbors..."

"The Yens. Paula and Wo Yen."

"The Yens haven't requested my help. They might not appreciate my interference."

She nodded, reaching out and clasping my hand. "Thank you so much for your help, Naida. Will you let me know? After?"

"Of course."

I watched her leave with a feeling of dread. Something wasn't right there. And I really hated to walk into situations not knowing what I was walking into.

A chill wind blew through the store as the door eased closed behind Alissia. It hit me with the force of a hammer between the eyes and left a deep, disorienting ache behind. I grabbed for the counter-top, my fingers white as I clutched it in an attempt to keep from succumbing to the usual vertigo.

The connecting door opened, and Sebille came into the bookstore from the artifact library. "I brought the book."

As usual, Sebille had clearly felt the wave of magic hit. Sprites were especially sensitive to magic waves, which was why she made a perfect assistant to me, an artifact keeper who didn't always know how to read the waves my artifact wrangling orders arrived in. When an order arrived, if I couldn't figure out what it was for, Sebille would confer with her mother, Queen of the Sprites and other local Fae. Between them, they could usually help me find the source of the trouble.

I took a deep breath and eased myself onto my stool, the world still spinning around me.

Sebille settled the Book of Pages onto the counter. "I'll make tea."

My assistant had a way with tea that eased the effects of my magic overload. I thought she inserted a little Sprite magic into each cup, but she insisted she was just tea-talented.

Whatever it was, her tea usually helped ease the pounding headaches a summons to locate an artifact created and made it possible for me to do my keeper work.

Moments later, Sebille handed me a fragrant cup and I grasped it like a lifeline, lifting it to inhale its familiar floral scent before taking a tentative taste.

By the time I'd finished the tea, my headache had eased to a dull throb. I reached for the book, but before I could open it, a soft, adorable form leaped onto the counter and sat down on the leather-bound tome, a pair of round, orange eyes narrowing in concern. I leaned into Mr. Wicked as he purred and rubbed against my face.

"Hello, little man. Where have you been?"

"He was snooping around in the back," Sebille said, giving my cat her usual glance of distrust. "I've caught him trying to play with SB twice already this week."

SB was an artifact, a parrot that once belonged to Blackbeard, the pirate. He was inextricably linked to the sword which lived safely out of reach on a top shelf in the artifact library.

"How did that go over?"

Sebille gave a mean little chuckle. "Not so well. The parrot might have surpassed his bleeping quota for the month in just those two attempts."

SB was actually short for Sewer Beak because of the salty language the bird tended to spew at every available opportunity. His swearing was so bad that the previous keeper had put him under a magical bleeping spell.

"It's a good thing Wicked can't talk," I told Sebille.

My kitten cocked his head, reaching out to smack me gently on my cheek. Fortunately, no claws were involved, so I assumed it wasn't meant as a reprimand, merely a playful tap.

Though there was something in his gaze that made me wonder.

"What was the sorceress here for? Did she buy that book on spelling failure away?"

I stared at Sebille. Had I mentioned my thoughts about the book and Alissia to my assistant? I didn't think I had. An uncomfortable feeling swept through me. Sometimes I worried the Sprite could read my mind. And given how often I thought bad things about her...she *was* very annoying...that was a terrifying thought.

"She wanted to report a possible artifact poisoning."

Sebille looked suitably alarmed. "Was it for the artifact order that just arrived?"

Unlike most "orders", mine didn't come via mail, email, phone call, or even through a magic mirror. Unfortunately, my orders arrived via painful delivery from the universe, and were mostly undefined, leaving me to use any means at my disposal to figure out what, where, how, and why all by my lonesome.

As you can no doubt imagine, it had been a haphazard system at best. If I hadn't had Sebille and her expert research methods with the communicating mirror artifact in the library, I'd have spent a lot of time aimlessly searching and probably never finding anything. If I knew what I was looking for and got close enough to it, my keeper magic would find it.

But I needed to get close enough first.

I knew there was something missing in my training. But, until I accidentally became the lucky owner of a Book of Blank Pages last month, I didn't know what had been missing.

However, I *did* know who to blame. The previous

KoA had been more interested in the next journey she would be making and not so concerned for preparing me for the work she was leaving behind.

Someday I was going to give her an earful. But that was an ambition for another day.

Shrugging in response to Sebille's question, I scooped Wicked off the book and ran my hand over the leather before opening it. "Let's find out." I placed my palm flat on the first blank page. "Show me the new order."

Without the frantic page flickering that had accompanied my first experiences with the book, when I'd had no idea how to use it, a picture oozed up from the page.

When the picture was complete, Sebille and I both squinted down at it.

"Is that...?" Sebille asked, frowning.

"Berbie!" I exclaimed happily. Under its surface of dents and rust, the well-known magical VW bug was barely recognizable. But I'd know the magic racing car anywhere. After all, Berbie had been the inspiration for my own VW Bug.

I ran my finger lovingly over the image of the famous car's faded white paint and chipped racing stripes, murmuring, "Don't worry, buddy. I'm coming to save you."

"You're such a derf," Sebille mumbled across the counter.

3

UPIDSTAY OGSFRAY EGSLAY

*W*hen the artifact I'm searching for is a car, they're generally pretty easy to find. They end up in junkyards, impound lots, or sitting in a tow yard somewhere waiting for someone to claim them. In most cases, they've been protected and cared for properly for the duration of their existence, so I don't receive the order to take ownership. But sometimes owners died or were unavoidably pulled away, and artifacts fell into the wrong hands.

That was when I got the order to reclaim them.

Never before had I been so excited to find an artifact as I was that day, when I pulled into the gas station on the corner of Rune Street and Divination Drive and saw the rounded form of the little car I was looking for under a filthy tarp behind the building.

One hooded eye peeked out from under the tarp,

its chrome surface pitted with rust and the bulb underneath yellow with age.

It made me sad.

The man inside the garage clearly had no magic in him. He had no idea what was parked behind his brick and wood building and no curiosity for anything except proof that I had a right to take it off his hands.

He looked down on me, probably six feet two inches and three hundred meaty pounds of belligerence with a lot of untidy hair jutting from his rigid jaw. "I ain't lettin' the property go until I see ownership papers."

I fought frustration. I could hardly tell him the magical universe had chosen me to rescue Berbie from the man's meaty, judgmental clutches. "I only have a verbal request from the owner's son. He lives in Las Vegas and can't come get his mother's car for several weeks. He wanted me to keep it safe until he arrives."

The man curled a bristle-covered lip. "It's perfectly safe out there under that tarp. Now get. And don't come back unless you have paperwork. I'm a busy man."

I settled a doubtful gaze on the phone sitting on his counter. The man had been launching angry-looking birds at green and pink, ball-shaped pigs when I came through the door. Sighing, I realized I'd have to use a little keeper magic on him.

Now, you're probably thinking I had something really cool at my disposal. Like a magic web that would hold him in place while I got the car and left. Or maybe something that would turn him into a zombie who only wanted to please. But, alas, my keeper superpowers really only gave me a couple of options, neither of them very useful unless I got really creative.

I didn't think it would do me any good to curl the guy's hair. Especially since he was bald. But my second superpower might do me some good.

Eyeing the door marked, "Restroom" in a short hallway at the back of the store, I lifted a hand and tugged my keeper energy forward, sending a thin stream of it into the man's pudgy middle.

He jolted when it hit him and frowned, looking momentarily perplexed. Then, without another word, the station owner turned on his heel and rushed toward the restroom in the back.

I headed out of the shop and around, hurrying toward Berbie. "I'm here, buddy," I assured the little car as it quivered beneath the tarp.

The lids clanked upward, showing me the rolling yellowed gaze as the car bounced happily on its springs like a frisky puppy. I tugged on the tarp, and it slipped part of the way off, catching on a bent piece of trim that caused the little car to shudder.

"Oops, sorry," I told him. "Let me just see where we're stuck..." I walked around the car and carefully unwound the fabric from the loose metal strip, grimacing. "How did you get in such bad shape, buddy?" I asked him, running a hand comfortingly over the rust-pocked surface.

Berbie responded with a soft purr of his engine and then belched black smoke from his tailpipe, the chrome covers on his front lights lowering with embarrassment.

"Not to worry," I reassured him. "Gas happens."

"Is that the right one?" Sebille asked me.

I turned to find her standing a few feet away, her ridiculous striped socks all but glowing in the sunlight. I had no idea why anybody would put glow stripes in knee socks. But then I had no idea why anybody would make striped socks in the first place.

I nodded, grinning. "Sebille, meet Berbie, star of television and the big screen."

Berbie bounced on his springs and honked twice in greeting, his cloudy lamps brightening with happiness.

Sebille narrowed her iridescent green gaze. "He doesn't look like a star."

Berbie seemed to deflate. I glared at her. "Be kind, Sebille."

She shrugged. Compassion was *not* her super-power. Or even something she vaguely recognized. "We need to get going before that unkempt guy finds out what you're doing."

I yanked Berbie's door open, causing a long,

drawn-out creaking sound. "Can you do something with that tarp, so he doesn't notice?"

Sebille nodded.

I closed the door and ran a hand lovingly over Berbie's dust-covered dash. His engine rumbled happily underneath the cracked leather seats. "Let's go, Buddy."

I sent a jolt of magic into him and sat back, grinning. Despite the fact that I'd devoured the already ancient Berbie movies when I was a kid, I still wasn't quite prepared for Berbie's enthusiastic departure. His engine roared, the front tires leaving the ground as Berbie did an extended wheelie that took us all the way to the street.

When all four tires hit the ground again, I turned to see that Sebille had magicked the shell of a small car and thrown the tarp back over it. She was climbing into my sweet little bug as Berbie took off with a screech of rubber on asphalt.

All I could do was hold onto the wheel and squeal with a mixture of terror and joy.

Berbie was happily ensconced in the artifact library, holding court with Casanova's chair, Shakespeare's desk, and SB, with a side of curious kitten to round off the gang. I was in the bookstore, documenting Berbie's retrieval in my keeper's Journal.

Sebille was spending a lot of time in the library, which was unlike her at that time of day, and I was starting to suspect she was more interested in the personable little magical car than she was letting on.

The thought made me grin.

I glanced up when the front doorbell jangled and nearly winced.

It was Alissia again. I realized that I hadn't followed through on her previous visit and felt a flush of quick guilt flooding me.

The sorceress hurried across the store in my direction. "Naida!"

Her expression was filled with alarm. I snapped my journal closed and came around the counter. "What's wrong, Alissia? Are you all right?"

She took my hands, squeezing them with her own cool ones. "It's Wo. He's taken a turn for the worse."

Guilt turned into a poisonous viper in my breast. "What do you mean? Has he hurt his wife?"

Alissia shook her head. "No. At least, I don't think so." She expelled a rush of frustrated air. "I just don't know. But he came to Mythic Specialty Teas today and demanded that I sell him the store. When I told him I had no intention of selling my store to him or anyone, his face went all...scary, and he threw some gold coins at me." She shuddered at the memory. "I had to close the doors and lock up, Naida. He threatened to come back tonight with the papers to sign Mythic over to him."

Tears filled her eyes, and the hands that clasped mine were shaking. "I can't lose my shop, Naida. It's my life. But I'm afraid that Wo will do something terrible if I don't sign those papers."

"This doesn't sound like the man you described to me," I said, frowning.

"It's not. That man is gone. I'm afraid he's let greed get the best of him." She shook her head. "I don't know what's happened to make him this way, but even his wife is frightened of him now. I can see it in her eyes."

I didn't know what to say. My hands were tied. For whatever reason, I hadn't received an order on the artifact Wo held. I didn't even know what it was. It was totally outside my purview to take it from him. If I did...basically going rogue...I'd get no magical protection from the authorities that controlled my orders. I'd be on my own against a power I didn't understand or recognize.

"I wish I could help, Alissia..."

Her fingers tightened on mine. "Please, Naida! Can't you at least meet him? Maybe the artifact will recognize you. Something's terribly wrong with him."

I had to agree. Generally, when an artifact creates such evil intent in the person who owns it, I get an order to remove it from their possession for the good of those around them.

I finally nodded. "I'll come. And I'll bring Sebille with me. Maybe she'll recognize the problem."

Relief softened the worry lines between Alissia's eyes. "Oh, thank you, Naida. Thanks so much! I knew I could count on you."

After some discussion with Sebille, along with the unwelcome and inflexible opinions of my resident ghost witch, we decided to bring Mr. Slimy along with us. Rustin was adamant that it sounded like we were dealing with a trickster artifact and I would need his protection because they could be very dangerous.

Sebille, understandably, and not surprisingly given her naturally cranky personality, took umbrage to his implication that she couldn't protect me. "I don't think she needs a frog sidekick to deal with an artifact," she said snottily to the frog sitting in the middle of the backseat.

Mr. Slimy just sat there, puffing out his throat and blinking slowly in her direction. I pressed my lips together to keep from grinning. I wasn't sure what Rustin was playing at by disappearing into the frog for the trip to Wo's Chinese Restaurant, but if he was trying to make my assistant look silly, he was doing a darn fine job of it.

There's nothing like being dissed by a frog sitting in a car to put a serious crimp in your day.

My stomach rumbled as we drove up to the restaurant and parked along the curb on the opposite side of the street. I stared at the usual tacky red and gold décor, taking a moment to appreciate the fire-spitting dragon mural on the wall closest to the long, front window. The decadent aroma of Chinese food was thick in the air, forming tantalizing fingers of enticement to tug me toward the restaurant's gaudy door.

"I don't know how Alissia works next door to this place without eating constantly," I told Sebille as I scooped up the frog and stuffed him into a small basket I'd gotten to cart him around in.

"I just remembered it's after lunch and we haven't had a lunch break." Sebille gave me a wicked look. "I believe I'm owed a lunch break."

I couldn't agree more. "Since we're really just here in an advisory capacity, I don't see why we can't get an egg roll and some hot and sour soup while we're here."

Sebille happily clapped her hands together. She even reached out and took the frog in the basket from me. "Here, let me help," she said.

I arched a suspicious brow. "Why? Are you planning on sneaking Slimy into the kitchen while I'm not looking?"

"Ribbit!" The basket wobbled on its handle as the weight-challenged amphibian made his outrage known.

Sebille gave me wide eyes. "Ixnay on the ogsfray egslay oksjay," Sebille said as a hazy mist seeped through the holes of the small basket.

Rustin stood facing us in the street, hands on hips, and stormy blue gaze raking my assistant. "You don't think I understand igpattonlay?" he asked Sebille.

She sniffed haughtily, stepping around him and heading for the restaurant. "How should I know? You didn't seem to understand English in the car a few minutes ago."

The ghost witch gave me a pleading look, and I rolled my eyes. "Will you two stop fighting, please? We have a potentially tricky artifact to wrangle. You won't be any help at all if you're fighting like toddler siblings."

Rustin fell into step beside me as I hurried after Sebille. "She's going to turn my frog bus into an appetizer. I think I have a right to object in a most strenuous way."

I grimaced. "First of all, ew! And secondly, nobody's making ogsfray egslay out of Mr. Imyslay." I grinned at my little pig-latiny ordway ayplay. "We're here to observe and assess a potentially dangerous artifact."

"And eat egg rolls," Sebille added with a glare for the ghost witch.

"And eat egg rolls," I agreed.

It was Rustin's turn to roll his eyes at us. Though, to be fair, it didn't have nearly the effect coming from him as it did from Sebille.

Showing disdain was another one of Sebille's superpowers.

The wave of delicious scents hit me right between the eyes when Sebille opened the door. I inhaled deeply, closing my eyes as I let pleasure roll over me.

I heard Sebille sigh happily beside me. "Please goddess this place isn't being run by a mad man. I need it to exist for the rest of my life."

"Amen and amen," I agreed.

Rustin shook his head, crossing his arms over his chest. "I'm going to snoop around while you two stuff yourselves."

"A perfect plan," I told him happily.

We stood beside a podium of light-colored wood near the front door and looked around. The place was packed to the brim, every table and booth within view of the door filled with eagerly munching customers. From the looks on their faces, the other people in Wo's were just as excited about the food as Sebille and I were.

"Is this a food enticement artifact?" Sebille asked, looking worried. "A magical egg roll? If so, I'm volunteering my services to taste all the egg rolls until I find the right one."

"Har," I told her as a petite, dark-haired woman approached us from the back of the restaurant. "Hello," she said, smiling. "How many?"

"Two," I told the hostess.

"Ribbit," Mr. Slimy chimed in.

Her brows lifted, and I laughed. "He doesn't need a chair," I joked.

"Maybe a high chair," Sebille murmured.

The woman frowned. "Is that a frog?" She asked quietly, as if she didn't want anyone else to know we'd smuggled a fat amphibian into the restaurant.

"Yes. But he doesn't eat much," I told her.

She dropped the menus she'd grabbed for us back into the slot at the back of the podium. "I'm sorry, we can't have live animals in the restaurant."

Sebille's hand tightened on the handle of the basket. I felt her energy before I saw it, reaching out in panic to stop her before she blasted the pretty hostess across the room.

Nobody. And I mean nobody, gets in between Sebille and an egg roll.

But she simply smiled and said, "Yes, you can."

The hostess blinked.

Sebille said, "These aren't the drones you're looking for."

The hostess blinked again and then smiled brightly. "Hello. There are two of you?"

"Yes, Sebille said. There are two of us." She gave me a wide-eyed warning look as if she thought I was going to belch out a confession about the frog in the basket.

There was no chance of that. I was just as susceptible to the allure of a crisp golden egg roll as the next guy.

4

GIRAFFE'S LEGGINGS

I swallowed a bite of moist, succulent egg roll and gave my assistant a look. "I should turn you in for unnecessary magic use against a human."

Looking smug, Sebille picked up her third egg roll. "A. You won't because you were an accomplice. 2. You're not that big of a hypocrite, and C. Don't be an idiot."

I knew she was right. I was sitting on the razor edge of being both a hypocrite and an idiot, and I was definitely an accomplice.

Besides...egg roll.

Sebille and I shared a grin and bit into our ill-gotten gains.

A haze settled over our table. I panicked briefly, and then realized the haze had great hair and judgmental eyes.

Rustin settled into an empty chair and crossed his legs, looking around the room with interest. "I've never had Chinese food before," he mumbled almost angrily.

"Seriously?" Sebille asked, her eyes wide. "Do you live in a cave?"

Rustin shrugged. "A frog, actually."

I snorted out a laugh, spitting egg roll chunks through the ghost witch.

He glared at me.

"Did you find anything?" I asked, wiping my mouth.

"A giant safe. In his office. It's like something you'd see in a large bank. Way overdone for a neighborhood restaurant."

I felt my eyes go wide. "Upper level weird. Like, caterpillars trying to decide if they need a Mani or a Pedi level weird."

Sebille grinned at the image I'd conjured.

"Did you slither through the door and look inside?" I asked, not realizing how insensitive the question was until he lifted his brows, oozing outrage through his airy pores. I winced. "Sorry. I'm still getting used to your unique situation."

He sighed. "I don't slither through walls, Naida. I'm not a ghost...in the specific sense of the word. So, no. I couldn't look inside. Not until someone opens it up."

I shrugged, eyeing the hostess. She greeted

everyone with a smile, but her manner seemed strained. "Do you suppose that's Mrs. Yen?"

Sebille sat back in her chair, her hands on her full belly. "Could be. Do you want me to find out?"

"No." I had no idea what Sebille might do to discover the woman's identity, but I figured she'd already done quite enough with the whole, "These aren't the drones you're looking for" schtick.

The woman caught me looking at her and hurried over. "Is something wrong?" I noted the way her small hands twined together and the worry lines between her brown eyes.

"Not at all," I assured her, giving her a smile. "The food was delicious."

Sebille nodded. "Best I've had in Enchanted."

The lines briefly disappeared as the woman smiled. "Why thank you. That's so nice to hear."

"Are you the owner?" I asked, trying not to notice the way the ghost witch had risen out of his chair and was close-skulking the poor woman.

"I am. My husband and I own Wo's."

At the mention of her husband, the woman frowned again.

Or maybe it was the icy breath of the frog rider against her skin. She reached up and brushed a hand over her cheek, turning toward the hovering specter with a confused expression. "It's cold over here, isn't it?" She asked softly. "I'll go turn down the air conditioning."

Glaring at Rustin, I reached out and stopped her with a touch on her wrist. "That's not necessary. We're very comfortable."

She looked down at my fingers and tensed. I pulled my hand away. "It looks like you do a good business," I said. "How long have you been in this location?"

The woman's gaze shot toward the door, her fingers twining nervously. "Almost five years now." She got a nostalgic look on her face. "I hadn't thought about it recently, but I can't believe it's been that long."

"You must make a good living," Sebille said unartfully.

The owner's face tightened. "That's really none of your business." She swept away from us, her posture stiff.

"Well, well," Rustin said, watching her push through the kitchen door. "I'll be right back."

I looked at Sebille. She was digging something out from between her teeth. She blinked in surprise at my stern glance. "What?"

"Really? You must make good money?"

She shrugged. "It was going to take you forever to find out what was going on at that rate."

Something crashed to the ground in the kitchen and, a beat later, the woman came flying out, tears sliding down her pale cheeks.

A tense silence descended on the dining room,

and everyone watched as she ran up the stairs at the side of the big room, slamming the door at the top.

Rustin suddenly appeared. "Let's go."

I reached for my water glass. "I just need to pay..."

He reached for me, his hand like ice against my skin. I was always shocked when his touch felt real because I did think of him as a ghost, rather than the magical embodiment of his spirit. "We need to go now!"

Sebille shoved to her feet. "Just throw some money on the table..."

The kitchen door slammed open and a small oriental man with wild eyes and a very large knife in his hand stood looking at us.

I didn't like the way he was staring at me as he started forward.

Apparently, I wasn't alone because the tables nearest ours suddenly emptied, the people finding reasons to visit the restrooms, leave the restaurant, or huddle in front of the register at the front of the eatery.

I stood up, my chair banging against the floor as I surged to my feet. I tugged my small stores of energy forward, holding my hand behind my back as Wo Yen stormed in my direction with a meat cleaver in his hand.

I looked into the man's eyes and icy dread filled my chest. Madness speared the brown depths of them, his expression murderous as he stomped closer.

Rustin slipped between Mr. Yen and me, and Sebille tugged her magic forward, flinging it into the room at large like a fistful of fairy dust.

Immediately, everyone went very still, the place falling into a deep, unnatural silence. I glanced around and saw that their gazes were blank and they stood in suspended animation.

Sebille had made sure none of the humans saw what was about to go down.

Rustin, Sebille and I turned back to the enraged restaurant owner. He'd stilled in mid-stride, the cleaver lifted into the air in front of him.

"We can't leave him there," I told my friends. "He might take that rage out on somebody else."

We thought about that for a beat, and then Rustin said, "There's a walk-in freezer in the kitchen."

I glanced at him, frowning.

"We can lock him in there and call the police when we leave."

That was as good a plan as any. There would be plenty of witnesses to tell the Enchanted Police that Yen had been threatening and aggressive. Though they wouldn't find the objects of his aggression. We'd be gone.

"That'll work..." I started to say.

"Well, I'll be a pair of Giraffe leggings," Sebille murmured. "He's breaking through."

My gaze whipped toward Yen. His outstretched foot twitched, and his enraged gaze shifted slightly.

In the blink of an eye, the man burst from the confines of Sebille's spell and started forward again. He lifted the cleaver higher. "You can't have it! It's mine!" Spittle flecked his lips as he charged me, the light glinting off the deadly edge of the blade.

He swung wildly in my direction and I jumped sideways, barely escaping the cleaver.

I held up my hands, energy spitting from my fingertips. "Mr. Yen, you need to stop right there."

When Yen swung again, the blade slicing through the sleeve of my loose shirt, Rustin swung a hand toward the chair I'd vacated, sending it flying to slam into the man's legs.

Yen went down, the cleaver clattering to the floor.

He didn't stay down long. He shoved the chair, propelling it with supernormal strength into my shins.

"Arg!" I yelled, falling across the table and sending dishes clattering to the floor.

Yen had his hand on the cleaver and was shoving off the floor before I even had a chance to straighten. His compact body hit me with such force the table broke underneath us. In the blink of an eye, he'd pressed the razor-sharp edge of the cleaver against my throat.

I looked up into the face of madness. Insanity roiled through the man's brown gaze. My hands pressed ineffectually against his shoulders.

It was like trying to move a thousand-pound boulder off my stomach.

"It's mine," he growled out. Rage turned his face purple and made the hand that held the deadly blade tremble with barely restrained violence.

"I don't want it," I told him, going very still. At that point, I think I was still in denial about the extent of his loss of control. Something in my brain kept telling me he was just sending me a warning.

Even when bright, sharp pain burned across the spot where the blade had settled beneath my skin. "I'm an artifact librarian," I said softly. "I'm just making sure everything...and everyone is all right. I didn't get an order. I'm not here to take the artifact."

He blinked and something that looked a little bit like understanding flickered through his gaze.

But it didn't last long.

He shifted slightly, hand tightening on the cleaver.

I gasped as his movement drove the blade deeper.

Rustin's ethereal face suddenly appeared close to mine. "The book, Naida."

I slid my gaze to him without turning my head. "I don't have it."

It slowly floated into the air beside me, a wispy hand beneath it. "Hurry. I don't like the grip this artifact has on him."

I couldn't disagree with that. Slowly moving one hand off Yen's quivering shoulder, I lowered it, touching the leather cover and feeling it warm and roll beneath my palm. The book opened, and I realized I had no idea what to ask for.

A mini-tornado to blow him away from me? No. Too risky with a blade to my throat.

"Sebille?"

Rustin shook his head. "She's busy."

I couldn't imagine what she was busy with but I sighed. My gaze slid to Rustin.

He shook his head. "I'm currently inside his brain trying to neutralize some of the poison. I can't sustain that while helping you with the blade. Use the book."

Well, that explained why Yen hadn't already lopped off my head.

I considered several other options, dismissing all of them as being too dangerous for the people in the place.

Suddenly Yen's head snapped up and his gaze flew to Rustin, widening.

Rustin's gaze widened too. "He sees me!"

"That's not possible."

Yen gave an enraged cry and shoved away from me, swiping at Rustin with the cleaver. "Mine!"

The deadly blade severed Rustin horizontally, his top half lifting off his bottom half. I screamed at the sight. But Rustin quickly reassembled himself with a frown. "That was annoying."

A hysterical giggle rose in my throat.

Mistake.

The sound brought Yen's attention back to me. I tried to shove to my feet, but I didn't have time.

The cleaver whispered through the air, headed right for my chest.

I slammed my palm into the book and yelled, "Outside!"

The blade cut the air, efficiently slicing through the spot where I stood.

Fortunately, I wasn't standing there anymore. I was outside the restaurant next to Sebille and Rustin, watching the madman with the cleaver turn the broken table and dishes into tiny chunks of debris.

I blinked, my heart pounding in my chest. "That was close."

Rustin crossed his arms over his chest. "You really need to get faster with that book."

I gave him irritated fish face. Then I turned to glare at Sebille. "Where were you?"

She swung a hand at the collection of people standing on the sidewalk. Behind them, sirens and the telltale red and blue flashing lights of the Enchanted Police roared up the street and squealed to a stop at the curb. "I was busy."

She'd gotten everyone out of the restaurant and called the police.

"Okay. I guess you're forgiven."

She rolled her eyes. "What about the artifact? Clearly, it needs to be under lock and key."

I nodded. "We'll hang out until the police get him out of there and then we'll go find it."

5

FLOUNDERING IN IGNORANCE

*a*s it turned out, we never got that artifact. When we entered the empty restaurant after the police left, we headed for the kitchen.

The door opened as we approached it and we slammed to a stop, looking into the tear-stained face of Mrs. Yen. She didn't look happy to see us. "We're closed."

Sebille opened her mouth, probably to say something insensitive and non-compassionate because that was how she rolled.

I hurried to cut her off, knowing the woman had to be in a delicate place at the moment. "I'm Naida Griffith."

The woman paled. "The keeper of the artifacts?"

I nodded, my gaze narrowing as she clenched her hands into fists and took a step back. "I can't let you have it."

Her reaction was odd. The artifact she apparently held had ruined her marriage, harmed their business, and most likely destroyed her husband's life and reputation. I wondered if the poison of it had already infected her. "You need to hand it over, Mrs. Yen. That artifact is dangerous." I prayed she didn't ask me for my orders.

She shook her head, taking another step back. "I need it."

"I know it's very seductive..." I started to argue.

She blinked, and then surprised me by laughing. "Seductive? Not in the least. The horrible thing has ruined our lives. But..." She flushed with embarrassment. "I don't have any money. I need it to bail my husband out of jail and get a lawyer."

I held her gaze, wondering how good an actress she was. Could she possibly be unaffected by the artifact? Probably not if she'd spent much time around it. "I don't think that's a good idea."

She seemed to force herself to calm, stepping toward me, though I saw the lines of strain on her attractive face. "I know this thing is dangerous. Believe me, I do. I'll just use it quickly and then turn it over. I don't want to end up like..." Tears slipped down her cheeks. "Poor, Wo." She hiccupped a sob, shaking her head. "I don't know if I'll ever get him back."

I glanced at Sebille. Predictably, she was shaking her head no. I knew rejecting the woman's request would be the safest option. But I got the sense she was aware of the danger and wouldn't risk becoming infected.

Still... "I really don't think..." I started to say.

Her face turned shrewd. "My lawyer will want a copy of your order."

Oh, belly-button lint from a cyclops. That was an unfortunate development.

Mrs. Yen cocked her head. "You don't have one, do you?"

I tried to look intimidating. "I can get it for you..."

"Good," she nodded. "As soon as I see the order I'll hand it over. In the meantime, please leave the restaurant. We're closed."

Sebille and I headed for the door. My assistant threw a glare over her shoulder. "You want me to give her the whammy?"

I assumed the whammy was what Sebille had done to the other patrons in the restaurant. It was tempting.

I sighed. "No. She has rights. I just hope she survives exercising them."

"Keeper?"

I stopped at the door and turned.

"I'll bring it to you as soon as I use what I need. You have my word."

I shook my head. "I'm not sure your word will be worth much once that thing gets hold of you, Mrs.

Yen."

I hadn't thought the woman could grow much paler than she already was, but I wasn't entirely surprised when she proved me wrong.

Our butts were barely in the car before Sebille was reaching for the mirror.

"What are you doing?" I asked as the street behind me disappeared. The long, blaring accusation of a horn sounded as I nearly pulled out in front of someone.

Sebille pulled an "oops" face. "Sorry. I need to talk to my mother. You should have gotten an order on that artifact."

I'd been thinking the same thing. If the position of keeper had been created to accomplish anything, it was to save innocents from the unexpected evil influence of rogue artifacts. I just kept thinking about Berbie that morning. The little car had been neglected, but he wasn't at risk. And he certainly wasn't in danger of harming someone else. The third option wasn't even worth a thought. Berbie would never reveal himself to a non-magic user.

He'd been around the track a few too many times for that.

See what I did there? Around the track? Snort!

"Ribbit," Mr. Slimy said.

I glanced at the frog in Sebille's lap. He stared back at me, slow-blinking as his throat puffed and depuffed. He wasn't amused.

Everybody's a critic.

I thought about the Berbie situation. Why had I gotten the order for Berbie but not for the artifact that was creating madness in the Yen home? One was time-sensitive and one wasn't. I should have gotten the Yen artifact first. Actually, I probably should have gotten it days or weeks ago. If I had, Wo Yen might have been saved from artifact madness.

Something wasn't right.

I tugged the mirror straight again and continued pulling out into the street. "You're right. And we do need to talk to Queen Sindra. But let's go there in person."

My lips curved into a smile as I thought about a visit to Lea's greenhouse. "She doesn't live miles and miles away anymore."

Sebille eyed me. "You just want to go check out those fruit trees."

I didn't deny it for the obvious reason that she was right. I did want to check out those trees. Two fruits. One stone. Or, something like that.

A few minutes later, I tugged open the metal door to Lea's greenhouse, walking into an enormous space that was several times the size it looked from the outside.

I blinked in surprise. I was pretty sure the space

was even bigger than the last time I'd been there. "Lea?"

A rustling sound came from the middle of the hothouse, where half a dozen small trees were clustered together. Those trees hadn't been there the last time I'd come for a visit.

The trees had dense, meandering branches filled with vibrant green leaves and brightly hued fruit. Though they spread wide, they looked to be only about as tall as Lea was, probably so she could easily tend them.

Her round, pretty face popped up in between two branches and she was grinning. "Look! Aren't they just the bee's ankles?"

Behind me, Sebille snorted.

I forced myself not to smile. Apparently, Lea's misuse of slang terminology was not only inaccurate, it appeared to be inaccurate across history. "That's a blast from the past."

She emerged from the cluster of healthy trees with two large, fuzzy orbs in her hands. Each peach was coconut-sized. "I was picking these for you. Sindra said they were ready."

My lips spread in a grin as wide as hers. "Look yonda, sweet Rhonda!"

Lea giggled like a schoolgirl. The branches above our heads rustled and I looked up to find Hex sprawled over a wide limb, her gaze narrowed sleepily.

Behind my back, Sebille rolled her eyes. I couldn't see it, but I could feel the vibration of it in a wave of negative energy. Not really, of course. But imagination is a wonderful thing.

"I'll find mother," the Sprite said in a voice filled with disgust. She popped into her bug size with a flash of light and buzzed toward the back of the greenhouse.

Lea hurried over, handing me a peach. "Your ears must have been burning."

Running an admiring hand over the fuzzy fruit, I said, "Huh?"

Lea lifted her peach-bearing hand. "We were just talking about you, and here you are."

"We're here for a much less happy reason than these fruity works of art, I'm afraid."

Lea's smile slipped away. "What's wrong?"

"We just came from the site of an artifact poisoning. One person down and another queued up to fail."

"Oh no," Lea bent down and placed the peach carefully into a wide but shallow wicker basket with a handle. "How did it get missed?"

That was my friend's diplomatic way of asking if I'd screwed up. While that was still a possibility, I didn't know how I could have. Although the migraines I get when a magical artifact order comes in are a pain in the...well...head, they do ensure I don't miss any orders. "I never got the order for it."

Two large bugs, aka Sebille and her mother, buzzed up to us and settled on the handle of the basket. Sindra was dressed in her usual queenly robes that matched her vibrant pink, purple and neon green butterfly wings. Her waist-length dark red hair was braided down her back and her pale face looked worried. "This is terrible," she told me, sounding too much like her daughter for my comfort. I could usually count on the queen to be the voice of reason and calm, the complete antithesis of Sebille, who was ready to do battle at the drop of a hat.

"What could have gone wrong?" I asked the queen.

Sindra and Sebille shared a look, and I realized they'd already discussed it. That irritated me a little, but they certainly had the right to talk about whatever they wanted, as long as they filled me in on the stuff that affected me.

"I'm starting to think we have a larger issue going on here," Sindra told Lea and me. "First the misappropriated frog incident..."

She was referring to Mr. Slimy. He and the magical book of pages arrived in my queue despite the fact that they really weren't a case of artifact retrieval at all. They'd been redirected to me to ensure that Rustin got the help he needed in time.

I frowned. "You think that was part of the same problem?"

"I do," Sindra said, buzzing up off the handle to hover in the air between Lea and me. Unlike her daughter, who was perfectly happy to sit in the vapery for hours-on-end observing people and finding ways to create chaos, the queen had trouble sitting still for more than a few seconds. "Something's gone wrong with the order system."

I hoped she was wrong, mostly because I had no clue what I was doing half the time. If the people who called the shots were clueless too, the magical artifact world was headed for a whole mess of trouble. "Has that ever happened before?"

I expected Sindra to shake her head. To my surprise, she nodded. "Yes. Once. About five hundred years ago." She grimaced, looking a lot like Sebille. "The Dark Rages were an unholy mess. It took the Powers That Be a hundred years to straighten out."

My stomach sank. "A hundred years?" Was that Whiny Wanda voice really mine?

"Yes. They waited too long. Which means we need to jump right on this before it gets too tangled up."

"How do you propose we do that. I have no idea who the Powers That Be are. Do you?"

Sindra shook her head. "Not specifically, no. We don't deal with them directly. I deal mostly in rumor and conjecture fed by experience."

"Awesome sauce," I mumbled. "How am I going to fix this when I don't even know where to start?"

"That's the easy part," Sebille finally said.

I looked at her as if she had three noses. "Easy? How?"

"You start with the frog squatter. He managed to get his case sent directly to you before. He must know at least one of the Powers That Be."

6

GRUDGE MATCH

"*I*s this because I couldn't save you from the frog?" I asked the ghost witch.

Rustin fixed me with an irritated look. "I told you, I don't blame you for that."

"Then why won't you tell me who you know at the PTB?"

He sighed. "I promised I wouldn't tell anybody about her."

I let my eyes go wide. "Her? I just need a name, Rustin."

"A name won't get you even close. Do you think the PTB live down the street? Do you think they shop at the local grocery store, wear flesh-colored yoga pants and dye their hair green?"

I grimaced. "Hopefully not. Those flesh-colored tights are disturbing on so many levels."

He shook his head. "I can't help you find her, Naida. I'm sorry."

"Then I'll just have to go to Madeline."

Even for a spirit, he looked paler after that threat. "You don't need to bother her with this..."

I forced myself not to grin. "Apparently, I do."

"Naida..."

I flipped a hand into the air. "No, that's okay. I'll respect your promise to the PTB not to out her. Even though she might be involved in ruining a family's life." Not to mention putting my favorite magical racecar at the center of an artifact mix-up. I was becoming more and more convinced that Berbie wasn't meant to have been confiscated by me. I only hoped the mix-up wouldn't keep him from his true destination. The fun little car deserved his happily ever after as much as anybody did.

The whole thing was turning into one big nightmare.

I started toward the artifact library, only to be blocked at the dividing door by a dour-faced ghost witch. "Madeline will blame me if you intrude."

I lifted my brows with not-so-feigned indignance. "Intrude? I've known your aunt for years, witch. She and I have done business together. I'm offended at your implication."

"If auntie agrees to meet with you, it's okay. But she doesn't take kindly to those who presume to have the right to approach her uninvited." He watched me carefully, no doubt trying to figure out if his words were having the desired effect.

He was trying to scare me.

I wasn't easily scared.

Okay, maybe I was. But I just wasn't smart enough to do anything about it.

Harsh, I know. But unfortunately, true.

I shoved through the door and headed across the library, ignoring the chill of his presence behind me. As I approached, Berbie's lids popped open, and his refreshed eye-lamps sparked with excitement.

I smiled when I saw him. The time in the library had all but rejuvenated the little car. The rust spots were gone, his racing stripes were vivid against his freshened white paint, and, judging by the way he was bouncing as I approached, his undercarriage was even springier than before.

I stopped beside him, running a hand lovingly over his revitalized surface. "We're going to get you back where you belong, buddy."

The little car's driver's side door snapped open, and his engine roared. Grinning wickedly, I threw Rustin a final glance. "Tell Sebille I'll be back in time to close up the store."

His response was to glower at me, crossing his arms over his chest. "You're making a big mistake, Keeper."

"Yada, yada, yada," I murmured in response. Then I climbed behind Berbie's steering wheel, settled into a buttery leather seat, and sucked in a gasp as he honked twice and took off like a rocket ship toward the oversized door at the end of the building.

One of the things I'd noticed when I'd brought Berbie back to Croakies was his magical navigational system. It had no doubt been disguised as some kind of enormous dial back in Berbie's early days of fame, but I recognized it for what it was as soon as I saw it.

As Berbie navigated the steep, winding roads through the mountains that surrounded the little town of Enchanted, I touched the fingertip reader in the center of the dial and watched a map and menu pop up. "Please state your target," a snotty English-butler-type voice told me.

"Madeline Quilleran."

The map disappeared and a face materialized. I recognized the long, aquiline nose, carefully combed-back hair, and tightly pressed thin lips as the owner of the snotty voice even before he spoke. "That location is not allowed."

I smacked the dial. "Madeline Quilleran."

The butler sneered at me. "Violence won't gain you that location. It is not allowed."

"On whose orders?"

The butler's head bobbled slightly as if he were shrugging. I leaned closer, trying to see behind him to see if he was actually standing somewhere. I couldn't see anything except the silver metallic back of the dial. "The Powers That Be have ordained that this location..."

"...Is not allowed," I finished for him, earning me an even deeper scowl from the disembodied butler. I sat there for a moment, thinking.

The butler stared at me, making me feel self-conscious and rushed. Then I had an idea. "I have a new location."

The butler inclined his bodiless head. "State your location, please."

"Maude Quilleran."

The map reappeared, and I got a quick glimpse of the Enchanted Forest before snotty butler reappeared. "I'm sorry, that location is..."

"Not allowed," I murmured, tuning him out. There had to be a way... I reached out and placed my hands on the steering wheel. "I could use a little help here, buddy."

Berbie bounced on his springs and honked. The driver's side window opened and one of Berbie's windshield wipers bent away from the glass, elongated, and then curved toward the car as it snaked through the open window.

Seeing it pointing directly at him, the butler blanched. "I say..."

Berbie sprayed the butler right in the face.

Bluish liquid slid down the glass dome on the dial, but somehow the butler spluttered and scraped his arrogant face. "Stop that!" he bellowed.

"Location for Maude Quilleran," I repeated.

The butler's thin lips twisted.

"Berbie?"

Berbie gave him another shot.

The butler coughed and spluttered, a hand appearing again to clear his face. "That location is not..."

Spray.

"It's not avail..."

Squirt.

"I can't..."

Spray.

"Bloody hel..."

Spray. Squirt. Spritz. Spray.

"All right!" The butler had an oversized hanky in his hand and was mopping at his face. "Your requested location has been entered into the system. Have a bloody nice day."

I grinned, patting Berbie on the dashboard. "Nicely done, Berb."

I sat back feeling pretty proud of myself. I'd beaten the system. Or...rather...drowned it.

There was nothing like a little magical waterboarding to make a tough day a little brighter.

adeline Quilleran lived in a castle that looked like it came straight out of a Grimm's Fairy Tale. It sat on a hill in a part of the forest that was so overgrown the sun probably rarely found a path through the enormous trees to touch the ground.

Despite that, there was a mystical glade feel about the place, with a soft effervescent glow near the ground rather than actual sunlight. Flowers covered much of the open space with vibrant color and a sweet scent.

The road leading to the dark, imposing castle-like home wound through the trees with a muscular kind of intent, as if it had been deliberately built so as to confound and dissuade anyone from approaching the powerful witch's home.

The forest around Madeline's private little witchy retreat was heavily warded. The air was dense, the energy prickling against my skin. But the power didn't come from repelling wards. There was no sensation of spiders crawling over my arms or impending doom dogging our forward motion.

I suspected the place was thick with assessment wards.

Madeline was taking our measure, sizing up her foe, and when we arrived she would be ready to deal with us as needed.

A mile from the house, I started noticing the enormous, ugly birds sitting high in the branches of the imposing trees.

Turkey vultures if I had to guess. But their eyes were red and their observation too intense to be mere birds.

They were Madeline's forward watch.

If I'd had any doubts before that she knew we were coming. The sight of those fearsome creatures' blood-red gazes keeping track of our approach would have quelled them.

I started to worry that I'd bitten off more than I could chew.

Several times I'd had to stop myself from telling Berbie to turn around. I had a deep sense that I was endangering more than just myself. Berbie was a magical artifact that had been placed under my care. It was irresponsible of me to risk his life on such a foolhardy errand.

In direct contrast to my own thoughts and feelings, Berbie seemed unaffected by the impending-doom flavor of our surroundings. The little car bounced over a tree root on the rutted road, hitting the ground again with a rev of his engine and an extra little leap just for the sheer pleasure of the experience.

I couldn't help grinning.

"Almost there, buddy," I said, reassuring myself rather than him.

Instead of making Berbie happy, my comment seemed to make the little car droop. His tires slowed a bit, and the metal antenna sticking up from his rounded frame sagged.

He was enjoying the trip too much to relish the idea of arriving at our destination.

I rubbed his dash. "But we'll have the whole trip home once I'm done here."

Berbie perked back up, even giving a short toot of his horn as we rounded the last curve and nearly ran smack into the enormous, black fortress.

Berbie screeched to a halt, his tires skidding a few feet before his bumper came to rest against the low rock wall surrounding the place.

I sat in silence for a long moment, watching the sky bubble and boil with the huge bodies of the vulture guard we'd passed along the way. By the time they'd all settled into position, the entire contour of the multi-peaked roof was lined with the things. They sat dark and silent against a patch of bright blue sky, the glow of their gazes a spooky and threatening contrast to the unexpected brightness of the sun.

They were very still. Hundreds of eyes staring right at us. Even Berbie finally seemed to catch the import of that ominous presence.

I opened my mouth to tell him to turn around. We'd just leave. Cut our losses. I was pretty sure Berbie could outrun the vultures if they attacked.

Kind of sure.

There had to be another way to get to the Powers That Be.

The dark line of the vulture guard shifted suddenly against the sky, wings lifting and heads cocking to fix their bloody gazes on the round-topped door in the center of the big house.

The door opened slowly, as if its sheer weight slowed its movement.

My stomach twisted with nerves as I waited to see what was on the other side of that door. My heart pounded against my ribs.

I struggled to breathe.

Beneath my butt, Berbie shifted, unsettled. I wasn't sure if it was my unease that was finally getting to him, or the combined power of the vultures and the strain of anticipation from that opening door.

The door disappeared into the darkness behind it and I saw the faint shape of something standing there.

Her form melted into the darkness, part of the shadows but not entirely a component of them. I watched in horrified anticipation as Madeline stepped from the house and stopped just outside the door, her malevolent yellow gaze finding me behind the windshield and locking on.

I could feel her displeasure like hot coals against my skin.

I held my breath against the prickling pain of that rage. Afraid to blink. Afraid to breathe.

She was taller than I remembered. Younger. With chiseled cheekbones that looked sharp enough to cut paper and piercing yellow eyes that glowed in the low light in front of the door.

She wore some kind of black dress, the fabric simultaneously sparkly and muted, as if it constantly tested the magic-drenched air and shifted according to the mood and purpose there.

She stood with her hands clasped before her, the thick black curtain of her hair dancing softly on a breeze that didn't seem to move anything else around her.

Come, Naida.

The words were in my head. They scraped against my brain like the physical embodiment of anger. Sandpaper words that left my head throbbing even as my limbs began to move.

I reached for the door and tried to wrench it open. Berbie gave a little warning toot and revved his engine.

The door wouldn't open.

He was going to turn around and leave whether I wanted to or not.

Goddess save me from an opinionated, protective car.

"It's okay, buddy. I have to go in now. We don't

want to make her mad..." I thought about that for a beat and then added, "...er."

After another moment's hesitation, the car door opened beneath my hand and I climbed out. I stood beside Berbie for a beat, staring at the witch.

A soft rustling noise drew my gaze upward. I watched as the vultures lifted their wings and then settled them back again, performing a strange ritual that seemed all too much like something I'd seen once at a baseball game.

"You presume too much, Keeper."

My gaze shot back to Madeline's. "I'm sorry. I know this is an imposition. But I have a dire situation, and I need your help."

Something in my voice, or maybe my determined delivery, must have appealed to the witch. After a tension-filled moment and more rustling above our heads, Madeline finally inclined her chin, looking for all the world like a queen.

As I started toward her, I only hoped she wasn't one of those royals with an unfortunate affinity toward razor-sharp blades dropping from great heights, removing the heads of people who annoyed them.

Because she looked pretty darn annoyed at the moment.

7

UNIVERSALLY RECOGNIZED

I gave her a smile as I approached, feeling it ping off her dour demeanor like a flea off a Rhinoceros's hide. "Thank you for seeing me."

She narrowed her startling yellow eyes. "This is a one-time exemption, Keeper. Do not presume to come again."

I nodded.

"How did you find me?" The question was so sharply presented I feared for my little four-wheeled friend. I fought to keep from glancing toward Berbie.

Like the uber-powerful witch she was, Madeline didn't need me to say the name. Her keen glance slid toward the little white car, and she harrumphed.

Berbie bounced on his shocks and happily tooted his horn.

High above our heads, the vultures shifted uncomfortably.

"It's not his fault," I said quickly. "I made him do it."

Madeline shook her head. "Do you really believe I would harm Berbie the Loving Bug?"

I think I grimaced. I really had believed it.

Her expression softened, looking almost hurt. "Come. State your business."

The home was much less horror movie chic than I'd expected. Still, the castle theme from outside had made its way inside.

The floors were wide, glossy wood plank, covered in thick rugs woven with the thirteen symbols of health and happiness that were prevalent in witch-lore. The furnishings were heavy, ancient, and covered in practical fabrics with minimal padding.

An enormous stag head hung on the wall over a fireplace that had probably been designed during an era when burning wood was the only source of heat in a home.

The glossy, brown eyes of the deer head seemed to follow me across the room as Madeline led me to a matching set of upholstered chairs before the fire.

Despite the warmth of the day outside, the big, old house held a chill inside its thick walls and the energetically spitting flames in the big fireplace were welcome both for their heat and for the uplifting atmosphere they created in the solemn room.

I sank into the dainty chair, surprised at the way

it enveloped me in comfort. So much so that I suspected the chairs had been imbued with contentment magic.

As soon as Madeline was seated, the air above our heads swished softly and a huge, black bird landed on one of her shoulders. The raven's small silver eyes fixed on me and it cocked its head, throat working as if it would speak.

Madeline reached up and smoothed the side of one finger over its glossy breast feathers. The scary-looking bird leaned into the touch, clearly enjoying it.

She saw me staring at the raven and smiled. "This is Rasputin."

"Your familiar?"

She shrugged. "My friend."

Something about the way she said it made me think they'd had a long history together. But I wasn't about to start interrogating her about it. Not yet, anyway.

"What business did you need to discuss with me?" Madeline asked, frowning.

Apparently, the small talk portion of our program was over. "I think something's going on with the Powers That Be."

She stiffened, her eyes literally pulsing with yellow light, and sat forward, sending Rasputin into the air with an affronted caw. "What do you mean?"

"I don't know." I shook my head. "I think someone's either making mistakes or deliberately miscuing the artifact orders process. Today, I watched a man nearly kill somebody over an artifact, and I never got an order on it."

She seemed to relax, which I thought was strange. "Perhaps there were extenuating circumstances."

"And I got an order to pick up Berbie, but looking back, I don't think I was supposed to." I described the garage where he'd been and the total lack of prep for the retrieval. Generally, the PTB set preparations into motion to ensure that my retrievals went off fairly smoothly when they could. The only exceptions were the occasions when we were dealing with criminal types or an emergency recovery. I described the retrieval to Madeline. She stared into the fire, unmoving.

By contrast, Rasputin's unflinching, silver-eyed focus on me seemed nearly human. In fact, watching him sit quietly on her shoulder with none of the usual bird-like affectations or quivery movements, I couldn't help wondering if the raven was what he seemed.

My story wound down, and we sat in silence for a few beats. Then Madeline turned to me. "I'll look into it."

I blinked in surprise. I'd meant to ask for her help getting Rustin to tell me what he knew. I hadn't expected her to contact the elusive PTB Board herself. "Thank you. But I really just wanted your help with Rustin."

The hostile yellow gaze narrowed. "What about Rustin?"

"He must have worked with someone at PTB to get the book and Mr. Slimy sent to Croakies when it was technically not an artifact retrieval issue."

She tensed again. I swallowed hard and went on. Carefully. "I thought maybe the person he'd dealt with could help me figure out what's going on."

Or fall to my feet in a sobbing confession of his or her guilt.

I'd prefer the latter, but I'd take help in any form I could get it.

A deep voice interrupted my thoughts. "If you believe something is amiss at PTB, why do you assume Rustin is behind the mix-up with the Book of Magical Assistance?"

My gaze shot to the raven, shock making my pulse spike and all the spit leave my mouth. "Did he just speak?"

Madeline looked at me as if I were a few flakes short of a breakfast cereal.

"It's rude to talk about me when I'm standing right here," the deep voice said, followed by a very-unhuman-sounding *haw, haw* sound.

I cleared my throat. "Um, hey. Sorry, I didn't know you could talk."

The sleek black bird cocked its head. "Why ever

not? You can talk, Maddie can talk, Miss Maude can talk, why shouldn't a man of my consummate intelligence be able to talk too?"

Man? I frowned. The bird had a clear accent that I didn't think was just the result of it being winged and beaked. "You're right," I said, hoping to soothe its...erm...ruffled feathers. "I'm sorry."

"It is nothing," he mumbled, flipping a wing. Judging by the literal smoothing out of his ebony feathers, Rasputin seemed mollified. "You didn't answer my question."

I struggled to remember the question. *Oh, right. Rustin.* "You have a point. I don't really know the answer to that." I doubted the bird would take "I just have a feeling" too seriously. I was pretty sure birds didn't even have feelings.

Rasputin fluttered from the witch's shoulder, landing on a small table between the chairs.

Madeline glanced toward the raven. "It's well past time..."

Rasputin bobbed his sleek head up and down as if nodding. "It's not as if we didn't see it coming."

I looked from one to the other. "What did you see coming?"

Madeline studied me a moment.

"Go ahead," Rasputin told her, shifting from one foot to the other impatiently. "Tell her."

"I'm not sure that's wise."

"Wise or not, as you said, it's past time."

Madeline sighed. She leaned forward in her chair, her long fingers gripping the arms so hard the knuckles were white.

It was strange to see the powerful witch so discombobulated.

I held her gaze, waiting for her to tell me whatever it was that was so hard for her to vocalize.

"Would you like me to say it?" the raven spurred.

Madeline angrily lifted a hand as if to brush him away. "You shouldn't have been able to find this place," she said, her gaze locked on mine.

Fish farts. We were back to that, were we?

She didn't say anything more for long enough that I thought maybe I'd nodded off in the middle of her statement and missed an important part. "Um, okay. Why not?"

Madeline glanced at Rasputin, frustration thick in her expression.

"I did say I was sorry for coming..."

"Maddie's PTB," Rasputin growled out. He scoured his witch with a quicksilver gaze, his movements abrupt and stiff. "Her location is protected by the Universe. The fact that the Universe saw fit to send you to us..." He lifted his wings in a movement that looked strangely like a shrug.

"—means that the trouble you're seeing is much worse than anyone understands," Madeline finished for him, her expression grim. She finally looked at me. "And that you've been chosen as the vehicle for discovering and fixing the problem."

"Toasted Troll boogers," I murmured.

"Precisely," Rasputin said, bobbing his sleek head.

I wasn't sure if he was lamenting the fact that I was apparently the Universe's choice for locating the problem, or the need for someone to look into the issue at all.

To protect my delicate ego, I decided to go with Option B.

"You should know," Madeline told me. "I was the one who helped Rustin. I've been aware of a weakness in the system for a while now, but I have no idea where it's coming from or how deeply it runs."

I frowned. "But, if you interfered, weren't you part of the problem?"

She sighed. "I thought it was worth the risk. I'd hoped to see if the system caught the error and fixed it. Unfortunately, it didn't."

I had a horrible thought. "Were you..." I swallowed the words, certain they'd enrage the powerful witch.

Rasputin lifted his wings and danced sideways. "Maddie wasn't responsible for young Mr. Rustin's predicament."

"No," she agreed. "But I should have seen what Jacob was up to sooner." Twin lines of concern deepened between her eyes. "I failed the boy. I'm trying to make it right."

"And you have no idea who or what is behind the current problem with the PTB?"

"Not for certain, no," she told me, glancing toward the fire. "But it's past time to find out. And apparently the Universe wants you to help."

8

A GRYM AFFAIR

I was almost home, my mind spinning with what I'd learned, when my phone rang. I answered in a daze, forgetting to even look at the screen to see who was calling.

"Hello?"

"We have a really big problem."

I frowned, trying to place the voice. "Who is this?"

The person on the other end sighed. "It's Rustin."

Rustin? Calling me on the phone? "But how?"

"That's not important right now. What is important is that we're at Wo's Restaurant and... We need you here."

"We?"

"Sebille and me."

I pressed him for more information, but he just kept insisting they needed me there.

I disconnected on a sigh. "Berbie, change of direction. We need to go to Wo's Chinese Restaurant."

The little car revved its engine and took the next turn on one and a half wheels, leaving me clutching the dash and bracing for impact.

If I hadn't known deep down that he was magically capable, I'd have needed a moisture barrier for my panties on that one.

Wo's was empty and quiet. The front door was slightly ajar and when I shoved it fully open a bell jangled but nobody came out to greet me. "Hello? Mrs. Yen?"

Despite Rustin's assurance that I should just come inside, I couldn't shake the feeling that I was doing something illegal. Or at least slightly unethical.

"Is anybody here?"

The kitchen door finally opened and Sebille's head popped out. "In here. Turn the lock on the door before you come back."

My discomfort doubling, I reached back and turned the deadbolt, then headed quickly for the swinging kitchen door.

My mind replayed the sight of Wo Yen exploding

through the door with a meat cleaver clutched in one fist, and I shuddered.

I'd seen artifact poisoning before. Many times. But I doubted I'd ever get used to seeing the madness it left in its victims' eyes.

Sebille was nowhere to be seen when I pushed through the door into the small, stainless-steel kitchen. I was shocked by the disarray of the place. Judging by the restaurant, I'd expected tidiness almost to the point of OCD.

Many of the cabinets were flung open, their contents strewn around the kitchen. Food lay rotting on the countertops, puddles of water surrounded two big packages of meat that had probably been frozen. A meat cleaver like the one Wo Yen had brandished at Sebille and me was embedded in the wall near the freezer.

The stainless-steel freezer door stood open on the sidewall and mist surrounded the opening as the icy interior air met the warmer air of the kitchen. I started forward, jerking to a stop when a fat, green form hopped across my path.

Mr. Slimy. I redirected him away from the open freezer with my foot and then headed over to see what my friends were up to.

I stopped abruptly in the doorway, my eyes going wide as I saw the crumpled pile of something frost-coated on the floor.

Sebille crouched over the body, her hand skimming an inch above it. I must have made a small noise because she looked up, grimacing. "She called the store asking for you. She sounded frantic, but she hung up without telling me what was wrong." Sebille looked down at the frost-covered form. "She's dead."

My vision adjusted to the scene and I found myself identifying characteristics of the crumpled corpse. She had a sleek cap of dark hair that skimmed in frosted ribbons over pale cheeks. Beneath the dark bangs, the blank brown gaze seemed to stare right through me.

I covered my mouth to hold in a scream and my stomach roiled with sudden nausea. "Is that Mrs. Yen?"

The mist at the back of the freezer shifted and I looked into it, finding Rustin standing behind the body with a frown on his handsome face. His wire-rimmed glasses had a slightly frosty aspect, which seemed strange since he didn't appear to feel the cold. "Yes, it's the wife. She appears to have been locked in here."

I closed my eyes, remembering the woman who'd assured me she could handle the artifact and return it to me once she'd gotten help for her husband. I couldn't really blame her for wanting to do what she could for him. I'd have probably done the same thing.

Then I had a horrible thought. My eyes snapped open. "Mr. Yen?"

Sebille shook her head. "He's still in jail. I called to make sure."

"Did you tell the police about her?"

Sebille shook her head. "We were waiting for you." She stood. "If she's still got the artifact, you need to retrieve it. We can't risk it falling into anybody else's hands."

I nodded, realizing I wasn't thinking clearly. So much had happened in such a short period of time, my mind was scrambled.

I extended a hand and released my keeper magic, watching it slide from my fingertips and weave through the air like a thin, gray ribbon. The magic found the crumpled, frozen corpse and slid over her, diving beneath her form to search the entire body.

But there was no chime of discovery.

Sebille, Rustin, and I shared a look.

"The killer must have taken it," Rustin said, his sad gaze locked on the dead woman at his feet.

I swallowed hard. The last thing we needed was another human getting artifact poisoning. The whole mess was spiraling out of control.

Just to be sure, I sent my seeking magic through the restaurant, and even through the small apartment at the top of the stairs I'd seen Mrs. Yen climbing before her husband had attacked us.

The artifact was gone.

I dropped into a chair at a table in the back of the restaurant, nearest the kitchen. Sebille joined me, and we sat in silence for a moment. Rustin hovered nearby, his hands clasped behind him and his expression dark.

Finally, I lifted my head and told them, "We can't avoid it. We need to call the police."

The only problem was, not all the police in Enchanted were magic aware. In fact, only a few of them were. And only one detective. Sebille nodded. "I'll have mother contact him. Hopefully, he's available. I don't like leaving that poor woman in there. It feels wrong."

I couldn't agree more. But with a magical component to the murder, I just wasn't sure it would be a good idea to allow magic-unaware law enforcement into the crime scene. At least not without our guy overseeing them.

Wise Grym was probably used to being compared to the Grimm of television fame. But, judging by the persistent frown on his handsome face, I was pretty sure the comparison rankled.

Especially the third time someone asked him where his buddy Munroe was.

I mean, get a clue, people. A joke generally has a past-due date, beyond which it really starts to stink like spoiled milk in the sweltering summer sun.

Grym slid a dark caramel gaze my way as he moved into the kitchen, his tall, wide-shouldered frame seeming to fill the space and yank all the light in his direction, leaving all the other cops in shadow.

I'd only met Detective Grym one other time, when rogue magic had infected a pair of women's shoes, forcing the wearers to walk into traffic and be killed, just as their original owner, who'd been a witch, had died. The magic poisoned shoes had created a repeating cycle of death that had been nearly impossible to stop since the shoes kept returning to the same dress shop in downtown Enchanted after they'd done their dastardly deeds. It had taken me a while to find that shop.

Detective Grym hadn't liked that I'd located the shoes before he had and, judging from the frigid way he'd greeted me at Wo's, he still hadn't forgiven me for it.

Grym spent a long time in the freezer. When he finally joined us in the dining room, the detective excused the uniformed cops who hovered nearby, giving my friends and me distrustful glances.

He waited until the other cops had gone outside and then sat down at the table with us, skimming Sebille and I a look before casting a glance toward

Mr. Slimy in his napkin holder in the center of the table. "Frog legs today's special?"

Behind Grym, Rustin recoiled, lifting a hand to smack the detective upside the head.

"Rustin!" I barked out before realizing what I was doing.

When Grym narrowed his gaze on me, I smiled. "The frog's name is Rustin."

"Ah. A pet then?"

Rustin glared at me as I nodded. "The frog is a pet, yes."

He nodded. "I thought you had a cat?"

I blinked, surprised he'd even known about Wicked. "I do. They're best friends."

If he noticed I was keeping my responses short and limited in detail, he didn't show it. He was probably used to people being careful with him. "So how did you two find the victim?" He scrubbed a hand over the back of his neck and looked toward the ceiling, two lines appearing between his eyes.

He was probably wondering where the chill was coming from that was bathing his back. I pressed my lips together to keep from smiling. He couldn't see Rustin. Or hear him. But he could feel the cold of the fathomless dimension where Rustin lingered.

"We came to check up on her," I told Grym. "Her husband was arrested earlier today."

Grym nodded, examining his notes. "Artifact poisoning," he affirmed.

"Yes. I tried to retrieve the artifact earlier, but she refused to give it up."

He stared at me, his expression telling me he wasn't impressed. "Aren't you cleared for forcible attainment?"

"Yes. But her husband had just been arrested, and she had no funds..."

"That pertains to my question, how?"

I glared back at him. "It pertains because I didn't..."

The kitchen door opened, Two people in dark jackets and khaki slacks rolled a gurney through. Mrs. Yen's body was hidden inside the morgue bag but my mind kept picturing her as she'd been inside the freezer, with the light of life already long gone.

I averted my gaze as a wave of regret filled me. "I should have made her give it to me."

"Do you think that would have brought a different outcome for the victim?"

His cold, distant demeanor suddenly annoyed. I leaned closer, letting my irritation show in my expression. "Yes, I do think that *Mrs. Yen* might be alive right now if she hadn't had the artifact in her possession today."

"You think she was murdered?"

"Yes," Sebille said, though he was still looking at me.

Grym turned slowly to look at my assistant. The Sprite's belligerent expression didn't soften as he stared her down. Her shoulders were squared, her chin high. She looked every bit the Fae princess she was despite the mash of colors she wore; the fire-red braids, the ridiculous striped socks, and shiny red shoes that looked like they'd disappear if a house fell on her. "As you are already aware," she said in a tone-of-voice that spewed disdain, "Mrs. Yen was killed by someone with fairy dust. The magic signature is all over her."

While that information seemed damming on its face, it didn't necessarily mean a Fairy had killed her. Most Witches had fairy dust in their magical stores and would sell it to anyone who was willing to pay the price. It was a fairly common way to incapacitate a person.

But it did imply that someone with magic had killed her.

The detective didn't confirm her statement. Instead, he stared at his notes as if he were thinking about what she'd said. I suspected it was a tactic he used to make people he was interviewing squirm.

It couldn't have failed more. Sebille didn't intimidate easily.

Finally, he lifted his gaze back to the Sprite. "Do you recognize the signature?"

Her lips tightened for just a beat, and I thought she was going to say yes. But she shook her head. "It's nobody I know."

Magic signatures were like fingerprints. They

only helped if you had a suspect to check them against.

Grym turned to me, and I suddenly found the frog-butt-cootied napkins very interesting. He wanted to know if Sebille was telling the truth and I had no idea. Knowing her, it was entirely possible she wasn't.

I kept my gaze averted, but I could feel the force of his stare like a physical thing.

"Where is the artifact now," he finally asked.

I looked up and let my gaze settle on his. Something spread through my belly as I met that caramel gaze. Something that felt good and bad at the same time. "It's not here. We think the killer took it with him."

"What exactly does it do?" Grym pointed to his notes. "Other than make people crazy," he added.

"From what we can piece together, it apparently conjures pure gold in the form of coins."

"Gold coins?" He shook his head. "I haven't heard about a lot of those showing up recently."

I shrugged. "Maybe they're being doled out slowly so nobody notices. Or maybe they're being redeemed with someone who wouldn't report them."

Like a magical artifact pawn shop, I thought. Moving artifacts that way was highly illegal, but I sometimes looked the other way if the artifact did no harm. This time, though, if the shop was involved in passing the coins through, I wouldn't be looking the other way.

I made a mental note to visit my favorite artifact reseller.

"A Midas artifact," the detective said, grimacing. "Nothing poisons people like greed. Especially if non-magic humans are being targeted."

I didn't respond. There was no need. I'd had exactly the same thought.

Grym nodded. He seemed to be considering something for a moment. He shoved to his feet, looking down at me. "I need that artifact found. And when you find it, I expect you to bring me in. If what you suspect is true and this killer is targeting the non-magical with the artifact, people are in great danger."

"That's why we brought you in," Sebille told him, lip curling. Her attitude said that she thought he was asking us to do his job for him.

Grym laughed without humor. Like the bad Grimm jokes, he was probably also used to Fae disgust. The Fae didn't much like cops, magical or not. They preferred to create their own justice, and it didn't always fall within the parameters of people who trained under a specific set of laws and rules.

Fae law tended to be pretty harsh.

"I'll let you know when I find it. But the artifact stays with me."

He looked for a moment as if he was going to

argue but then seemed to think better of it, nodding. "Agreed, Keeper."

A fter Grym left, we stopped into Mythic Teas next door. Alissia was behind the counter, her dour glamour even more depressed and dour-looking than usual. As I approached her, I saw the red-rimmed eyes and tear tracks on her cheeks.

"You heard?" I asked the other sorceress.

She sniffed, nodding. "I was about to close up early. I can't believe Paula Yen's gone."

"I tried to take the artifact from her, but she insisted on keeping it after Wo was arrested. I'm afraid someone didn't want her to have it."

Alissia's gaze went wide. "You think she was murdered?"

"Yes." I didn't go into details. It wouldn't do Alissia any good and would only make her feel worse. "I was wondering. You said Wo Yen came here and threw some coins at you. Do you by any chance still have those?"

Her gaze flashed with guilt. "He took them back when I wouldn't agree to sell the place."

I continued to stare at her until she sighed. Moving over to the register, she hit a button and the drawer came open. She tugged a tray from the drawer and reached underneath, pulling out a small gold coin. "He missed one."

I took the coin, running my thumb over the engraved dragon at its center. "I'll give this back, Alissia. But I need to take it for a while."

She shook her head, rubbing her hands along her arms as she shuddered. "No. I don't want it back. Those coins have ruined the lives of two people I care about. I don't need that kind of ugliness in my life."

I reached out and squeezed one of her hands. "I'm so sorry."

She shook her head. "You've done nothing wrong."

"If I'd gotten here faster, maybe..."

"No. You were right. Without an order, you had no power over that artifact. Wo would never have given it to you. It was unfair of me to ask."

"Not unfair. You did what you could to help them. You were being a good friend."

She nodded as tears slipped down her cheeks.

I left a moment later, and Alissia locked the shop behind me. It would be a while before she got over the horror of what had happened next door. Unfortunately though, she'd been wrong about one thing. Giving me back the coin wouldn't save her from the ugliness. It was too late for that. She'd already been touched by it.

9

FIDGETY ARTIFACT

*S*ebille held the coin in her hand, her thumb caressing the raised form in the center as a soft green light bathed her palm. After a moment she let the magic slide away, shaking her head. "I don't recognize the signature. All I can say is that it's different from the signature on the body." She frowned.

"What's wrong?" I asked, seeing the indecision in her gaze.

"The energy has a different feeling to it. Familiar, yet...twisted somehow."

I thought about that for a moment. "What do you think that means?"

She sighed, handing the gold coin back to me. "I don't know. I need to talk to Mother."

I dropped the coin into an indentation in the

console between the seats. I didn't know how the poisoning happened with that particular artifact, but I had a strong suspicion it was dangerous to hold the coin too much, and I intended to limit my exposure. Just in case.

We rode in silence for a few minutes.

"What do you want me to do?" Sebille finally asked as we neared Croakies.

"We need to talk to Theo," I told her.

"At Enchanted Collateral?"

I nodded. "Detective Grym was right. Pure gold coins aren't exactly a normal way to pay for stuff, even in Enchanted. The Yens had to have been passing the coins through somebody to get cash."

Sebille nodded. "There can't be too many places that would accept a lot of gold coins without questions."

"Exactly. I don't see Theo asking a lot of questions, do you?"

"No." Sebille thought for a moment and then said. "We need to follow the inheritance trail on the artifact too."

I skimmed her a look. "I've got somebody working on that."

"Who?" Sebille's bright red brows lifted in surprise and a little suspicion. "Rustin?"

"No, but close." I hesitated only another moment before admitting, "It's Madeline Quilleran."

"Shut up, Shirley!"

I grinned. "Don't call her Shirley." Shirley the pixie, otherwise known as the Witch-epedia of the magical world, was decidedly cranky about being called by her Earthly name.

"How'd you manage that?" Sebille asked. "And how'd you find her? I thought her location was hidden by the Universe."

"It is, was, but apparently the Universe wasn't counting on Berbie the Loving Bug's magical navigation system."

Or his predilection for waterboarding the Nav guy.

"Maybe the 'verse wanted you to find her."

I didn't tell the Sprite that was Madeline's thought too. I needed time to consider what it all meant before I talked about it with Sebille. "Whatever the reason, we need to find that artifact fast. Before someone else gets hurt. Or worse."

Enchanted Collateral was a fancy name for Theopolis Gargantu's pawn shop. He'd picked the pretentious-sounding name because he believed it would draw more people into the shop. It seemed to be working. The place was almost wall-to-wall customers when Sebille and I walked through the door.

The bell that jangled to announce our arrival

was much louder than the delicate tinkling that sounded at Croakies. In fact, everything at Enchanted Collateral was "more" and bigger.

Like its owner.

Theo's huge head came up when the bell jangled. He turned slowly to see us standing there, his deep-set eyes widening. The big man grinned, showing crooked white teeth that were very large and very square in his wide mouth.

"Are you looking for something in particular?" asked a short, muscular woman behind the counter nearest the door. She had sun-reddened skin that looked like she'd spent too much time outside, nervous pale-blue eyes, and wavy brown hair. The clerk wore clothes which looked like they might have come off the "not so gently used" racks at Enchanted Collateral.

I nodded toward Theo. "We're here to see the owner."

Theo said something to the customer he was helping and touched the arm of a pretty young employee who was normal-sized but looked like a pixie next to Theo.

The young woman hurried over to assist the client Theo had been helping. She glanced our way, frowning slightly as I headed toward Theo.

The employee who'd spoken to us went back to whatever she was doing behind the counter, dismissing us almost rudely.

Theo motioned toward the back of the shop, where his messy office awaited his return.

Sebille and I threaded our way through the tangle of people and items, which covered almost every surface and clogged up most of the floor. Theo had created narrow aisles between the stuff that looked barely wide enough for him to move his massive bulk through.

Somehow he managed. Despite how human lore presented them. Giants were gentle and agile creatures. Especially given their size. A normal male giant, like Theo, generally stood close to seven feet tall and weighed four to six hundred pounds.

None of that bulk was fat. Every inch of Theo's big form was crafted from muscle over heavy bone. A formidable creature, Theopolis Gargantu was somebody you didn't want as an enemy. Fortunately, Theo was slow to anger and always quick to look for ways to help.

He waited at the office door for us, the grin on his face spreading nearly from ear to ear. "Naida keeper! How are you, girl?" Theo enfolded me in a wall of hard flesh that smelled like sugar cookies.

Giants have a strong affinity for sugar. Especially when it came in cookie form.

Maybe I had some giant in my hereditary pool.

"I'm great, Theo. You look good."

He blushed, his big hands skimming over his chest as if checking to make sure everything was in place. "Ah, thank you." He slid a shy glance over my assistant. "Hey, Sebille."

Sebille's characteristic annoyance fled her gaze, and she smiled. "Theo. It's nice to see you again."

I blinked, shocked by her strangely normal greeting.

Theo's cheeks flamed red. "Come in, come in." He threw open the door with a flourish and indicated we should precede him into the room.

I held my breath as I walked through the door. I hadn't been speaking metaphorically before, when I'd said his office slash living quarters awaited his return. A giant's residence was a living, breathing entity. An artifact. As such, it had a life of its own and you never knew what to expect when you walked into one.

Fortunately, like their owners, a giant's home artifact was generally kindly and benevolent. Less fortunately, also like their owners, the rooms tended to crave clutter and accumulations of stuff. And that clutter always seemed to be moving around.

One little thing about giants that human folklore failed to capture was that they were creatures of change. They loved change and sought it out at every opportunity, creating it themselves if it didn't naturally occur in their lives.

As I stepped through the door, a waist-high pile of magazines shot past, running over my toes on its way to a shadowed corner on the window wall.

I sucked back in time to keep from being bowled over by the paper tower, and then found myself dancing sideways as a chair squealed across the room and tried to shove itself under my butt. I fought it at first, and then realized my journey through the space would be much easier on the chair.

The only problem was that, like all the other furniture in the space, it was giantnormous, the seat hitting me in the middle of my back rather than beneath my butt.

I fell forward as the seat of the chair propelled me, dodging between a lamp that was turning to flash a welcome and an elderly vacuum cleaner whose wand shot toward me in a hazardous attempt at a greeting.

Something buzzed past my ear and I realized Sebille had taken the easy way out. She landed on the island-sized surface of Theo's desk and perched her tiny backside on a pad of stickies that were large enough for her to sleep on in her two-inch tall Sprite form.

I often wished I was able to use Sprite shrinking magic in the course of my day. But at that moment, with a body-sized throw pillow heading happily for my face, I realized the magic would be more than handy. It would probably save my life.

A large hand snapped out and grabbed the pillow from the air before it could literally smother me in love, and Theo looked sheepishly down at me. "Sorry."

I forced a smile. "Your rooms are very... perky...today."

He nodded, indicating a chair that I needed a stepstool to climb into. Fortunately, Theo had enough non-giant visitors that he had one handy.

Once I was seated in the middle of the hard-wooden chair, legs dangling and swamped by the furniture like a toddler, Theo dropped lightly into his desk chair and shooed a painting of the ocean away when it tried to fly over and greet us.

Sebille's tiny face had taken on an ashen quality as the thing headed right for her. In her small form, that painting would have literally squashed her like a bug.

"Tea?" Theo asked.

I shook my head, not willing to even think about how that would happen. My luck I'd get a swimming-pool-sized cup filled with hot liquid, and an over-exuberant creamer would fling me into it headfirst.

Theo waved off the tray of tea things heading our way. It banked to a stop and swung around so quickly the lid flew off the sugar bowl and sailed through the air toward Theo. He reached up and snagged it out of the air without breaking eye contact with me. "What brings you to Enchanted Collateral today, Naida?"

"I'm looking for an artifact."

He leaned forward, his gaze filled with interest. "You don't say? I'll help if I can. Can you describe it to me?"

Unfortunately, I couldn't. "I've never seen it. I only know what it does."

He nodded.

"It creates gold coins."

His gaze went wide. "Oh, my. But you have no physical description?"

"No. I'm guessing it's a small purse of some kind. It can't be a cash register, that would be too bulky." I thought back to Paula Yen's small fist clutching something I assumed had been the artifact.

"This artifact has already poisoned two humans and has disappeared again. It's imperative that I find it."

Theo shook his big head. "I'd help you if I could, Naida keeper. But I haven't seen anything like that. I'd tell you if I had."

Something in the deep-set brown eyes made me wonder if he would. A giant's predilection for collecting stuff was only matched by a dragon's hoarding ways. I wondered if the dual nature of owning something that constantly created more somethings might be too much for Theo to resist.

"What about your employees?" I asked.

Shaggy brows lowered over his eyes. "It's just the

two girls. Penny's so sweet and harmless. She'd never hurt a fly."

"Penny?"

"The prettier one of the two," Theo said with an uncomfortable glance toward Sebille. "Sorry. But it's true."

Sebille nodded. "What exactly does Penny do for you?"

He flushed. "She's good with numbers. She keeps my books and helps me organize my finances." His grin widened with pride. "She's going to be an accountant someday."

"Does she need money?" I asked, hating the way he looked at me when I probed.

"I pay my employees well, Naida keeper."

I'd inadvertently stepped on the giant's enormous but delicate toes. "I meant no disrespect. I have a job to do, and it's important. This artifact is hurting people, Theo."

He grunted. "Penny's in college, but she seems to do okay. She definitely appears to be flush with shoe shopping funds." His grin made me feel better.

Sebille snorted. "Who doesn't have enough money for another pair of shoes?" she asked.

Me, I thought crabbily. I couldn't remember the last time I'd bought new shoes. *How pathetic was I?* "And the other girl?"

I caught his quick frown before he squelched it.

"She's a little sharp around the edges, but Birte's okay. I help her out as much as I can."

Thus the hand-me-down clothing she wore. "Do you think she's capable of stealing?"

He hesitated a beat too long, but when he finally responded, he was emphatic. "No. She wouldn't. I'd stake this place on it."

I really hoped it didn't come to that.

"Has anyone come to the shop with gold coins to sell lately?" Sebille asked.

Theo rubbed his smooth chin in thought. "Gold coins? I'm not sure. A few coins have shown up. But mostly they were silver and a few copper."

"Like pennies?" I asked, losing hope that Theo could...or would...help us.

"Yes. They were a few decades old and worth some money but nothing like what you're talking about. I don't remember seeing any gold coins."

"You're sure?" I asked.

He hesitated just long enough for me to wonder how honest he was being. "I'm sure."

"Will you check your records for me?" I asked him. "You might have forgotten something that would help us."

His brows lowered in displeasure at my suggestion that he could forget anything about his beloved shop, but he finally nodded. "Of course. I'll help in any way I can."

"Good. Thanks."

"You might want to ask around too," Sebille suggested. "Your friends in the pawn business might have bumped up against this artifact. If nothing else they need to be warned how dangerous it is."

Theo nodded enthusiastically. "You're right, Sebille." He flushed as he looked at her, one big square finger twitching in her direction as if he wanted to touch her. "I'll do that."

"Thanks for your help," I told Theo. He nodded and I looked down, down, down toward the floor, wondering if I'd lose a few notches of respect if I fell on my face trying to dismount from the chair.

A big hand appeared in front of me. Theo smiled knowingly.

With a long-suffering sigh, I wrapped my fingers around two of his and let him lift me down like a child. I might have been better off falling on my face than for word to get out I had to be airlifted out of the giant's rooms.

I drove Berbie into Croakies a half hour later, after stopping to grab take-out food on the way home. Despite the dead body in the freezer, the lingering smells of the fried food at Wo's had given me a hankerin' for egg rolls.

Unfortunately, there were no other Chinese restaurants within twenty miles of Enchanted.

So we grabbed fish sandwiches at a drive-thru.

"Thanks, buddy." I left Berbie in the center of the artifact library, patting him on the bumper as I trudged wearily toward the stairs.

The little car happily tooted his horn.

"I'm going to call it a day," I told Sebille.

She nodded. "Me too."

I carried the paper bag of food in one hand and Mr. Slimy's plastic basket in the other. As I climbed slowly upward, I became aware of footsteps climbing the steps behind me and jolted to a stop. I whipped around, and Sebille jerked to a stop too.

Her eyes went wide. "What's wrong?"

I stared at her for a moment and lifted my brows in question.

"What, Naida?" She held up her hands, one of them clutching a paper bag that matched mine.

Then it hit me. My stomach twisted with alarm and dread. Stars burst before my gaze. I opened my mouth to say something...anything that would make it go away.

But I had nothing. "Oh," was all I could manage.

Sebille's bright red brows lowered over her iridescent eyes. "Did you forget I was staying here?"

Goddess, yes. I had! And I hadn't had any time to research a place for her to stay.

Stupid, stupid, stupid!

"Um, no. It's okay. It's fine. I...um...I think there's a cot down in the library. You can sleep there."

Sebille cocked a hip, glaring up at me. "Custer's cot? I don't think so, Naida. You know that cot makes you dream of his last stand all night. I have nothing against learning about history, but that's ridiculous."

I grasped at the only straw my clutching fingers could find. "It comes with its very own musket."

She lifted a brow at my pathetic attempt to talk her into sucking down the nightmares to sleep on that cot. "Nice try."

Desperate to head off what I knew was coming, I almost stomped my foot. Then I had an idea. "Your box! You surely have a bed in that thing, right?"

She grinned and started up the stairs, pushing past me. "I do. It's all up here. In your apartment."

That wasn't exactly where I'd been headed with my suggestion.

My first thought was that the Universe had pulled a fast one on me, flinging me into a giant's home as a really bad joke. But the furniture wasn't oversized. There was just *so much* of it. Like Enchanted Collateral, there were only narrow pathways around the stuff.

My wonderful — carefully decorated in the spare, comfortable style that I not only loved but couldn't live without — studio apartment currently looked like a used furniture store.

I couldn't even see *my* stuff. All I could see, in the sea of furnishings, were unfamiliar chairs, sofas, and tables, bookshelves filled with books, and no fewer than three curio cabinets which were chock full of vaping supplies.

"Where's my stuff?" I wailed before I caught myself and cleared my throat, striving for calm.

"It's in the back," Sebille said, looking unconcerned. "My stuff's prettier so I thought it should get top billing."

My mouth hung open, both from her audacity and from the sheer, blood-chilling reality of what I'd done. "You can't stay here." The words were out of my mouth before I even realized I was going to say them. But once they were out there in the universe, I didn't regret them very much.

Sebille snorted. "Funny girl." She headed down one curvy, narrow pathway that I think headed into my kitchen. I was so disoriented I wasn't sure where I was at the moment.

I hurried after her. "No, I'm serious. This isn't going to work."

Sebille worked her way past two kitchen tables and eight chairs to open my refrigerator door.

Well, at least she hadn't brought her own fridge.

Wait...two tables? My head whipped around like

a possessed teenager on copious amounts of pea soup. "Are you kidding me?"

Sebille pulled a bottle of water from the fridge, holding it up to me in question. I dropped into a chair at my table and let my bag of food hit the table. "Sure. Thanks."

"I couldn't decide which table looked best in here, so I left them both."

Rather than drink it, I held the bottle of chilled water against my forehead. "*Mine* looks best in here. All of *my* stuff looks best. I can't live like this, Sebille."

Something in my tone must have found the teeny-tiny kernel of compassion that existed deep, deep, deeply hidden in her frozen tundra of a heart. She sat down at her table and opened her paper bag, digging the fish sandwich and fries from its greasy depths. "Okay. I'll consider putting my table back into the box."

"And everything else. You can use *my* furniture for the day...two at most...that you'll be here."

She shook her head. "I need my stuff. It's not fair that you get your stuff and I don't."

What wasn't fair was me having to give up any of my space to a woman who'd rogue vaped herself into eviction and was trying to make it my problem.

I bit my tongue against that response, however. It even sounded petulant in my head.

"I'll compromise with you. Lose the table and

one couch." Who in the world needed three couches anyway? The woman had lived in a studio apartment. I couldn't even imagine how crowded it had been in there.

Scratch that. I *could* imagine.

I was currently living it.

10

NO ROOM IN THE INN

*I*t was a mean, hateful plot to drive me totally insane. How was it possible there were no apartments in Enchanted that fit the size and rent requirements of my picky assistant? I *had* to find her a place to live that wasn't my home. My sanity depended on it.

After a night of listening to her whistle-snore to the tune of Fairy in My Garden, I was beyond tired, maybe a tiny bit cranky, and ready to cut my ears off with a ritual knife. And that didn't even take into account the whole television control issue.

We'd started out arguing about which show we were going to watch. I'd finally pulled rank and grabbed the remote from her, tuning into my favorite paranormal sleuth sitcom, which I'd waited eagerly for *all week*.

Sebille had quietly fumed on her couch for

several minutes and then used her magic to duplicate the remote-control device, muting mine and taking control of the television before I could say, "Whoa there, unfair!"

I'd gone to bed early, so mad I couldn't go to sleep, and promised myself I'd find her a new place to live before I did anything else the next morning.

Then I'd lain there all night, listening to the Sprite's nose whistle.

I rubbed my weary eyes as the words on the computer screen in front of me wobbled and blurred.

I needed more tea.

I shoved to my feet and my head exploded. The pain was like a knife to my temple, slicing through bone to get to my brain and turn it to mush. I cried out and fell to my knees, my head bouncing off the thankfully padded arm of one of Sebille's many transplanted chairs.

What it was doing in the kitchen, I had no idea. I suspected it had something to do with my assistant staggering to the bathroom this morning from the couch where she'd slept.

Her couch, of course.

I rested my head against the chair arm as wave after wave of agony sliced through me. The pain clamped down on my lungs, making it impossible to draw breath, and sent prickles of discomfort over the skin of my entire body.

I tried to breathe through it, but I couldn't get enough air through my clenched lungs. Beyond my tightly clasped eyelids, colors flashed and spun, and mini explosions splashed a rainbow of light that made my stomach roil and pitch, sending glass and other debris skittering across the kitchen floor to pierce my skin.

A not-too-distant door slammed and a familiar voice called my name.

I couldn't respond.

A moment later, Sebille's hands found my shoulders, and she helped me into the chair I'd been leaning against.

Colors rioted against my lids. The acrid stench of something burning stung my nose, and Sebille's shiny red shoes crunched across the kitchen floor.

It seemed forever before the gentle scent of my assistant's special tea wafted toward my nose. I reached blindly for it, hitting the edge and spilling a burning dollop onto my bare knee.

The pain was a drop in the ocean of my overall agony.

Cool, gentle hands touched my fingers, guiding the cup toward my face. I tried to inhale and found I couldn't.

Sebille had been talking to me the entire time she was in the room. I heard the shape of the words but my battered brain couldn't make out their meaning. They were disembodied notes in a song I didn't recognize. She could have been speaking German for all I knew.

Warm wetness slid down my cheeks and from my nose. I suspected it was blood. The thought terrified me, but I couldn't think about anything at the moment except the immensity of the pain in my head, which had radiated down my throat and into my shoulders.

My muscles were so tight they were creating a secondary ache that felt like a giant Charlie horse.

The cup met my lips and I pried them open, managing to swallow a small amount of the hot liquid inside.

Several moments later, Sebille set the cup aside after having doused me with most of it. "Are you feeling any better?" she asked.

I pulled air into my lungs, relieved to finally get enough to ease the painful tightness in my chest.

"A little." My voice was tight, raspy, and didn't sound like me.

Though I could understand Sebille again, the pain in my head had barely eased from the tea. "It still really hurts."

Sebille placed cool palms on my temples and sent warmth into me. Her magic smelled like rosemary and lavender and eased a fraction of the pain in my tortured flesh. "Any better?" she asked a moment later.

My muscles slowly started to ease.

I nodded, laying my head back against the chair with a sigh. Though pain still jolted through me at irregular intervals, it had dulled enough for me to think. "Did you feel the wave?"

Silence met my question. If it wasn't for the sweet smell of her magic lingering in the air, I'd have thought Sebille had left.

I wrenched my lids open, cringing at the sunlight glaring off the stainless steel of my refrigerator.

Sebille was staring at me with a deeply worried expression on her face.

The sight of her concern made me want to fold myself into the fetal position and hide. "What is it? What's wrong?"

"We need to talk to mother."

Oh, oh. "You weren't able to identify the order in the wave?"

Her expression didn't soften. "Worse than that. I didn't even feel a wave."

"I t had to have come directly from the Universe," Queen Sindra said.

I frowned from beneath the hot compress on my head. "Yeah, my orders always come from the Powers That Be."

The tiny Fae queen shook her head. "You misunderstand, Naida keeper. This wave wasn't an order. It didn't come from the PTB. It came from the Universe, directly to you."

Sebille fidgeted beside me. I'd never seen her so discombobulated, and it was making me antsy. "Could you read the intent?"

Sindra sent her daughter a look that I couldn't interpret.

Whatever it meant, I figured it wasn't good news. "Tell me. I need to know."

Sindra buzzed closer and then away, her wings moving triple time above and behind her. I closed my eyes as trying to follow her rapid movements sent a fresh spike of agony through my brain.

"It was a warning," she told me.

"A warning about what?" Sebille asked, frowning.

Amazingly, Sindra shrugged. "I don't know. This message was meant to go directly to the keeper. That's why you didn't feel it hit, and why it hit her so much harder than usual."

She wasn't kidding. It had hit me like a herd of giants trying to get to the world's last two-for-one sale behind me. "That's impossible. I wouldn't have survived a direct message from the Universe."

Sindra's jewel-colored eyes narrowed. "You nearly didn't."

She wasn't wrong there. When I'd finally managed to drag myself into the bathroom and looked into the mirror, it was to find streams of blood running down my cheeks from my blue eyes and more blood coating my lip from my nose. I'd never bled from a magic wave before. And the pain in my head was still bad enough to make me nauseous, with no signs of abating, despite my having downed several cups of Sebille's magic tea elixir.

My apartment hadn't fared much better. Every piece of glass in the place had exploded into tiny pieces. My appliances had died underneath a massive surge of power, and every bulb in the place had shattered.

I shuddered at the memory of the devastation waiting for me when I returned to Croakies. Lea's sweet kitten, Hex wound her small, soft body around my ankles, purring loudly. I picked her up and held her against my chest, burying my face in her sweet-smelling fur. My pain eased a few notches, allowing me to draw a full breath for the first time since the wave had hit.

I regretted having left Wicked behind in Croakies. He'd been trying to get to me as Sebille all but carried me out of the place, and Sebille had shooed him away. He'd probably known he could ease the pain.

"But what good is a warning if we don't know what it's about?" Sebille asked, seeming more frustrated than curious.

"That's a good question, Sebille. I wish I had an

answer for it." Queen Sindra hovered before my face, looking worried.

If the Sprites were at a loss, I was definitely in trouble. They were key to reading any magic wave that pelted me in my job as KoA. The fact that they hadn't been able to read the wave that sent me to my knees that morning told me better than anything the wave had been different.

Which meant I couldn't respond to it the way I usually did.

I knew what I had to do. And in my current state, I wasn't looking forward to it.

I needed to go back to see Madeline Quilleran.

But this time, I was going to follow proper channels so I didn't find myself on the wrong end of a turkey vulture drubbing.

Reluctantly settling Hex onto the floor, I headed out of the greenhouse. I opened the back door of Croakies, stopping to let the heavy silence flow over me like a balm. As a keeper of the artifacts, I took strength and magic energy from the artifact library. It was my refuge. My safe place in the wild ride that was the world of magical artifacts. And it was as close to medicine for my soul as I could get.

I closed my eyes and inhaled deeply, pulling the combined scents of old wood, aged paper, and untold amounts of retained magic into my lungs.

When I opened my eyes again, I felt better.

"Meow!"

Mr. Wicked all but threw himself at me. I caught him mid-air and pulled him in close. "Hey, buddy." His purr rumbled in my chest and spread through me, easing the last of my aches away and sharpening my mind again. "Thanks for trying to help earlier."

Wicked shoved his head under my chin, his purr deepening. I kissed the soft spot between his dark gray ears and sighed. "I guess I have no more excuses for putting off what I need to do."

Holding my kitten close, I headed across the huge library, toward the ancient standing mirror located several yards from the dividing door into Croakies.

I situated myself in front of it and took a deep breath. Wicked rested happily in my arms, for once not in a hurry to get down and go exploring. The artifact library was an endless source of entertainment and busywork for the cats. Lea often brought Hex over so she could play and explore with Wicked.

I pulled my keeper magic forward and let it trickle through my fingers, settling my fingertips against the age-speckled glass and sending the gray pulses of snapping energy into it with a single thought.

Madeline Quilleran.

The energy blossomed in the glass and spread, looking like glistening gray spider webbing as it spread from side-to-side and top-to-bottom of the ancient glass.

As the last of the webbing met the antiquated wood frame, the pattern at the center began to fade, leaving clear glass in the form of a dark-haired woman I recognized even before her slender shape and pretty but sharp features eased into view. "Keeper. You've had some excitement."

I was debating how to respond when a commotion sounded behind her and Rasputin landed on her shoulder. The sleek black bird glared at me from the depths of the communicating mirror. "You need our help."

Delivered in a voice somewhere between his rich, human baritone and the raven he presented himself to be, the words still managed to make me shudder.

They already knew. What else about my life did Madeline and her daunting familiar know?

"I was hit by a massive power wave today..."

Madeline nodded. "The Universe. Yes. We felt it."

I blinked in shock. "You felt it? But how? Why?"

"The Powers That Be are attuned to Universal energy. It thrums through our veins at all times. Today, I felt a spike in that energy. We went looking for its source."

"And found you," Rasputin said.

I had a terrible thought. "So all the PTB felt it?" If Madeline's assumption was right and the deadly gold coin artifact was tied to one of the PTB, then whoever was responsible knew the Universe was waving at me.

She nodded. "Yes, but only I knew what it meant."

I waited for her to explain. She didn't disappoint.

"You reached out to me. You asked for my help. Every interaction between PTB and a magic ambassador creates a tentative bond. The bond will tie us together until we both sever it."

Terrifying. "Oh."

She smiled. "Don't look so horrified, Naida keeper. I only wish to help."

Rasputin fixed his beady silver gaze on me. "We must take steps immediately. If we don't, the Universe will wave at you again."

I clutched Wicked against my chest, dismayed. "That can't happen. I barely survived this one. And my home is trashed."

Madeline nodded. "Fear not. They'll give you time to recover." She looked at a spot to the side of the mirror and frowned. "Nine in the morning?" she said, a question in her voice.

Rasputin bobbed his head, his wings fluttering upward as she moved. "Yes. That will give us time to prepare."

They both turned to me. "We will arrive in this very spot at nine o'clock tomorrow morning. Prepare yourself. You'll be taking an arduous journey, and you will not be allowed to bring anyone along."

I clutched Wicked tighter. "I have to bring Wicked." I didn't know how I knew, but I was certain I had to bring my powerful familiar with me.

Madeline stared at my cat for a long moment.

Wicked stopped purring and stared back at her, his small body tensing with apprehension.

I was starting to wonder if I needed to protect him when Madeline finally nodded. "That is acceptable. Nine in the morning, Naida keeper. Until then."

Their image slowly faded out of the glass, leaving me with more questions than answers. Like, for example, how did I prepare for a journey when I had no idea where I was going and why?

I glanced longingly at Shakespeare's desk, wishing I had time to research the Universe and try to figure out what journey Madeline had in mind for me.

But I had a thoroughly trashed apartment to put back in order. I had work to do at Croakies. And I had a journey to prepare for, even though I had no idea what that preparation entailed.

11

TRUST NO ONE

*A*s I descended the stairs to the artifact library the next morning, I felt no better prepared than I had the day before. I'd spent the better part of the night trying to research the PTB and the Universe and had gotten nowhere.

I finally gave up and went to bed, figuring that I could at least get a good night's sleep to prepare for my journey.

I listened to Sebille's nose whistle all night. After a while, the cadence of the whistles started to appeal to my musical side, and I found myself humming Fairy in My Garden along with Sebille's snores, and finally lulled myself to sleep around three in the morning.

My eyes jolted open at eight. Four cups of tea later, I took a very hot shower, dressed in the black leather garb I generally wore when wrangling a particularly difficult artifact, and was heading down the stairs when the front doorbell jangled.

Sebille came into the library a few moments later, a concerned look on her face and a box from our favorite bakery in her hand. She eyed me up and down, one red brow arching. "You expecting trouble?"

I snorted out a laugh. How could I not? Lately, my life was defined by trouble, constantly challenged by it. Trouble could be my first, last, and middle names.

Though that would be boring. And my initials would be like something from a Roadrunner cartoon.

"Sorry," Sebille said. "Stupid question." She handed me the box. "I thought you might need sustenance before embarking."

It was my turn to arch a brow. "Sustenance? Embarking?"

She growled softly. "I've been hanging around my mother too much."

The Fae in Queen Sindra's court tended to speak a more archaic form of English when they were *in situ*. As a Sprite whose wings flapped firmly in the modern world, Sebille found the speech particularly irritating.

But then, almost everything was a particular irritation to Sebille. So...there was that.

"Do you have any idea what's about to happen?" Sebille asked me.

"I wish I did." I pulled a fat, glazed donut from the box and took a large bite. "Mfmpt Qfmrpts..."

Sebille held up a hand, and I swallowed.

Mr. Wicked bounded into the room, tail held high and paws smacking at a bug buzzing the air around his head. He ran over and fell onto my feet, immediately deciding my shoe strings were more interesting than the bug.

"Madeline Quilleran and Rasputin are coming here at nine this morning," I told her. "I'm hoping she can fill me in on what's going on."

"Okay. What do you want me to do?"

"Back me up when they're here? I'm pretty sure I can trust Madeline, but I'd feel better if you were watching my back."

"I can do that." Sebille leaned close and plucked a chocolate cake donut from the box. "In the meantime, I'll make tea." She disappeared back into the bookstore just as the bell over the front door jangled.

I sat down at Shakespeare's desk and attempted one more search. Wicked jumped soundlessly onto the desk and curled up on one corner, falling immediately asleep.

Placing my palms over the ancient, pocked leather of the blotter, I said, "Magical Universe, location and function." I'd tried dozens of variations on that theme the night before and had come up empty-handed. But, during the seemingly endless hours I lay awake, I'd decided that I needed to be more succinct in my request.

The ancient tooled leather boiled and rolled under my hands, working the request for a long moment. Just about the time I thought it was going to be another dead end, silvery light flared in the air above the desk, and a single sheet of paper drifted downward, settling onto the surface of the now, inert blotter.

I stared down at it, my mind struggling with what I was seeing. The sheet of paper didn't contain any of the information I'd requested. In fact, it held only three words that created more questions than answers.

Trust no one.

I grabbed the yellowed sheet of paper, turning it over to see if there was more on the back.

It was blank.

The missive was wholly represented by just those three words.

Trust no one.

Troll's flip flops! What in the goddess's best underwear did that mean?

Magic whispered behind me, and I turned to find the surface of the mirror roiling, a thick gray mist filling the space behind the ancient glass.

Wicked jumped up with a hiss, his orange gaze locked on the mirror.

I quickly shoved the warning into my pocket and turned to find a shape forming inside the mist. To my supreme shock, a slender hand shot out of the mist, followed by a long, shapely leg, and then Madeline Quilleran's head and torso eased out of the miasma.

She looked down her long straight nose at me. "Keeper."

I pressed my sweating palm over the paper in my pocket and nodded. "Hey..."

The mist exploded out of the mirror, and a tumbled mass of black feathers barreled out of it, hitting the high back of a velvet-covered chair with a muffled thump and sliding down into a feathery puddle on the seat.

Beak open and eyes rolling around in his head, Rasputin sprawled across the magical chair for a beat, wings akimbo. Then suddenly shot upward with a startled cry.

I hid my grin. "What's wrong, Rasputin?"

He settled down onto the top of the mirror's frame, his quicksilver gaze filled with affront. "That chair accosted me." He eyed my cat as if Mr. Wicked had been responsible for his being groped.

I let a grin curve on my face. "That's Casanova's chair. I'm afraid you're not special. It molests everybody."

Rasputin gave the rogue chair a raven-like glare and then adjusted his feathers, rippling from head to toe and then smoothing out as he pulled his dignity back around him. "This is a singularly strange place you have here, Keeper."

"Tell me about it," I murmured.

The chair bounced against the floor for a moment, its gilded arms waving happily, and then settled into inactivity again to stalk its next victim.

Madeline shook her head. "Ras, try to stay out of trouble, won't you? The fate of the world is hanging in the balance."

The bird looked disgusted. If birds could roll their eyes, "Ras" probably would have rolled his. "The fate of the world is *always* hanging in the balance. It's so wearying."

Madeline fixed her startling yellow gaze on me. "Are you ready?"

I briefly considered telling her I couldn't be ready because I had no idea what I was getting ready for...but then settled for a noncommittal nod.

She inclined her chin. "Good. We need a scrying surface."

I held out my hands. "Do you scry with water or Mercury?"

She frowned. "Sand, actually." Eyeing the mirror, she murmured, "Or glass, in a pinch." She nodded. "This will do."

I opened my mouth to argue. I didn't want her befouling my communication mirror with dark magics. But I realized as she placed her hands over the surface that she'd already done that when she'd used it to transport herself and her raven familiar into the library.

Madeline held her hands up, palms toward the mirror, and danced her fingers in the air as if playing a piano. Her lips moved in a silent spell.

The glass in the mirror started to soften. It wavered and rippled like water lapping against its frame. The center of the rippling glass stuck up above the surface of the mirror, like a fountain of water but formed of glistening granules instead.

I watched in fascination as the whole thing lifted from the frame and, when Madeline spun her finger, turned horizontal and hovered in front of her at chest level.

Madeline studied the undulating surface for a moment, tapping the air above it here or there, and changing the landscape with her touch. I was transfixed by the sifting sand, which rose into the air above the plane, and then folded over itself and sifted gently back down to puddle and roil around the base of each tiny sand fountain.

Sand rose in energized spurts across the surface, occasionally tumbling back to level again or shooting up in varying heights.

Mr. Wicked dropped to his butt next to my foot and watched the geyser show with deep interest, cocking his head with every new emission.

Through it all, Madeline studied the surface carefully, her expression intent upon her handiwork.

From his spot upon the mirror's empty frame, Rasputin's beady gaze moved back and forth between us, clearly wondering about my reaction to Madeline's magical handiwork.

I tried to keep my expression neutral, nearly biting off my tongue in an effort to keep from asking questions.

Sebille's heavy footsteps came up behind me and she handed me a cup of steaming tea, her brows arching at the show before her. "What took you so long?" I whispered.

She frowned. "Customers. You do remember we have an actual business to run, right?"

Her sarcasm aside, I *had* actually forgotten that for a moment. I'm blaming the drama that is my life.

Madeline ignored my assistant, but the raven eyed her like she was a tasty bug under his beak.

She eyed him back. "Don't even think about it, bird."

Rasputin's feathers shifted in a wave that crested at the back of his neck. "I beg your pardon?"

Sebille snorted. "Don't tell me the bird thinks he's superior to me?"

I shrugged. I was pretty sure the bird thought he was superior to everybody. "You'd feel better if you'd seen his arrival through the mirror."

The sleek midnight feathers rippled upward again, showing the pale down of their underside in his agitation. "I'd like to see you traverse the magic waves inside this old hag," Rasputin ground out in his snotty voice.

Sebille and I giggled.

"That's no way to talk about your mistress," Sebille said with a cocky smile.

Rasputin's head whipped toward Madeline and his beak came open on a squawk of outrage. "I didn't mean..."

Madeline didn't look at him as her fingers continued to walk across the scrying field, but I noticed her lips curving upward just slightly in the corners and I liked her a little bit better for it.

"I was referring to this elderly crone of a mirror and you know it, *Sprite*."

He said the word as if it were a rotted worm on his tongue, but Sebille only giggled more.

A purple puff of magic dust suddenly gusted from the middle of one of the sand geysers.

Madeline's fingers stopped dancing and she glanced at me. "Our path has been determined."

The smile died on my face. Reality smacked me right between the eyes.

It was about to get real.

With her scrying complete, Madeline finally skimmed Sebille a look. "Princess."

I didn't have to look at the bird to know the

witch's quiet deference to Sebille ruffled his feathers anew.

Sebille didn't grimace at the title as she usually did. She stiffened slightly and inclined her chin, looking for all the worlds like the royal personage she was. "Witch Quilleran. You'll have a care with my friend?"

I almost swallowed my tongue. Knowing Sebille the way I did, I realized she was probably just using the leverage she had at hand against what could be a formidable foe if Madeline should ever decide we weren't on the same side. But the Sprite had sounded just like her mother in that moment. And she'd placed me under the Fae's protection with her seemingly harmless question.

Madeline didn't respond for a long moment. It was clear she understood the import of Sebille's question. Finally, she inclined her head, a tight smile playing about her lips. "It is *her* journey, Princess. I'm simply helping her navigate it."

Sebille smiled, too, the meaning behind that smile clear. Whether Madeline agreed to keep me safe or not, Sebille would hold her responsible for my well-being.

Madeline lifted an arm and Rasputin fluttered over and landed on it. Then she looked at me. "You have the Book of Pages?"

I blinked in surprise. "Yes..." I tried to remember where I'd left it. I really needed to be more careful.

The book was a powerful magic tool, and I tended just to leave it lying around wherever.

It suddenly appeared in front of me. Sebille's gaze caught on mine as I reached for it, thanking her. She held my gaze for a long moment, a message buried in the iridescent green depths of her eyes. Then she nodded and stepped back. "I'll see you on the other side, Naida."

I didn't have time to ask her what she meant by that because the book flipped open and, as Madeline reached a finger into the tallest sand geyser on the scrying plane, the pages snapped to a stop on a fascinating depiction.

With a yowl, Wicked jumped into my arms and I dropped the book.

I felt the magic grab me top and bottom, and rip me out of my world before the Book of Pages even hit the ground.

12

MISTRESS OF THE UNIVERSE

I slammed into thick grass and felt Wicked fly out of my hands with a yowl. The impetus of my crash sent me skimming a good three feet on my face, the fragrant mix of broken grass and gouged dirt filling my nostrils.

I finally came to a stop and lay there a moment, groaning. "Well, that was just a slice of slug pie," I muttered.

Two slender feet appeared in front of my face, one pointed toe tapping impatiently against the thick grass. I looked up, squinting against the over-bright sun. Madeline Quilleran stood straight and tall, her black slacks and matching silk blouse unblemished by dirt and grass.

Obviously, she'd landed a bit better than I had.

Rasputin sneered down at me from her shoulder,

looking smug. "Now who's made a mess of her landing?"

That was the moment I realized I was definitely going to regret making fun of the bird.

I shoved to my knees, spitting grass from between my lips, and sneezed. Wicked rubbed against my side, purring.

Apparently, *everyone* had landed better than I had. *Hippopotamus halitosis!*

I stood, brushing debris off my jeans and tee shirt. Both knees of my jeans were green, stained with grass juice, and I had a perfect round dirt stain at the center of each boob.

Great. I had to save the world with dirt nipples on my shirt.

Awesome sauce.

Madeline arched a perfect brow. "Are you ready, Keeper?"

"Never more ready," I told her, trying to look enthusiastic. "I'm pumped."

Her lips tightened and I got the distinct impression she was trying not to smile.

Dang witches!

She turned on her heel and started off across a vast expanse of rolling grass. I fell into step beside her, frantically brushing at my shirt. Wicked ran ahead, happily pouncing on dandelions and swatting at butterflies in the flower beds.

I finally gave up trying to remove my dirt

areolas and lifted my head. A familiar structure loomed ahead. I skidded to a stop with a yelp. "No!"

Madeline turned to me with a questioning glance.

I couldn't believe it. "What are you playing at, witch?"

Her attractive features tightened at the disrespect. "Be very careful, sorceress."

My mind slid to the sheet of paper Shakespeare's desk had produced. *Trust no one.*

I pointed a finger toward the hulking structure ahead of us. "What are we doing here? I thought we were going to confront the Universe."

She inclined her head. "That's correct, Keeper. We are in the right spot."

I dropped my hand, anger making it hard to breathe. "The Quilleran castle? I don't think so."

I spun on my heel, calling out to my cat. "Wicked, come on."

"You don't want to do that, Keeper," Madeline said softly behind me. I turned, expecting to find her pointing something sharp or otherwise deadly at me.

She was simply standing with her hands clasped in front of her, looking worried. Then I remembered Madeline Quilleran, fourth level witch, didn't need weapons. Her hands were her weapon. "Or what?" I asked, my rage making me shake. "You'll blast me?"

A sudden horrified thought skimmed through my mind.

Wicked!

"What have you done with my cat?"

The worry lines between her eyes, which seemed more glowy than usual, deepened. "Your cat? I'm sure I don't..."

"He's over there, spazmastic," the bird said derisively. "Wallowing in the bushes." The raven shook its sleek head. "The creature has no sense of dignity at all."

I glanced toward the spot the bird had pointed to with his beak, seeing the rose bushes rustling and the tip of a light gray tail sticking out from between the spikey branches. Relief and embarrassment combined in my breast, bringing a flush up my throat and into my face. "Oh."

"Trust me, Keeper," Madeline told me. "This is where we need to be."

Trust no one...

I glanced at the house and then back to the witch, swallowing a ball of worry in my throat.

Or maybe it was a dirtball.

I really had no choice. I suddenly wished I'd brought Blackbeard's sword with me.

I sighed. "Okay, but I don't like it."

"Understood. All is not as it appears," she told me in a maddeningly ambiguous tone.

"Yeah, that makes me feel better," I muttered.

We started off toward the house again, Mr. Wicked finally joining us. He entertained himself by jumping at my shoelaces as I tried to walk. I grinned, reaching down to scoop him up and bury my face in his fur. "Don't scare me like that, buddy."

He batted my nose with just a tiny bit of claw, scolding me for asking him to restrain his *joie de vivre*.

We climbed the familiar curved stone steps to the front door, and Madeline lifted her hand as we approached. The door flew open, revealing the entryway where Sebille and I had almost been skewered by a hundred athames, a fireplace poker, and at least one sword.

Not to mention blown to smithereens by a posterior-load of blast traps.

Needless to say, I wasn't looking forward to going back in there. I held Mr. Wicked close, despite his unhappy wriggling to be set free. If anything happened this time, I wasn't accidentally leaving Wicked behind like I'd left Sebille and Mr. Slimy behind last time.

Unlike the previous time I'd been there, the entryway of the Quilleran home wasn't empty. An old man stood several feet from the door, his expression lacking any of the surprise I would have expected at our sudden arrival.

I wondered which Quilleran he was. I didn't know of any ancient family members in the area.

Maybe he was visiting from another country or something.

The ancient man stood bent and still, one long-fingered hand wrapped around the skull that formed the handle of a wavy wooden walking stick. His eyes were surrounded by a mass of wrinkles so prodigious they reminded me of one of those Japanese dogs whose faces consisted of just a bunch of flesh waves, lapping over one another.

The gaze ensconced within the waves of flesh was a deep, intense blue. His hair was a tangled yellow-gray mess that spilled over bony shoulders and merged with a scraggly beard of a slightly darker gray.

He inclined his head as Madeline strolled gracefully into the house and then skimmed a look my way, shaggy brows lifting at the condition of my clothing.

I fought the urge to cross my arms over my chest to hide my unfortunate dirt smears.

"Welcome," the old man said in a rich baritone that didn't seem to match his age and condition.

"Ulysses," Madeline said by way of greeting. "You know why we're here?"

The old man inclined his head. "The abyss awaits."

Wait! What? The abyss? Nobody ever wanted to hear that the abyss was waiting for them. That was just wrong. "Um, Madeline...?"

The old man turned and started toward the stairs. Madeline followed, Rasputin lifting off her shoulder to fly ahead of us, as if he couldn't wait to get where we were going.

Wicked yowled with irritation and raked a claw over my hand to make me release him.

I stood rooted to the spot as my kitten bounded up the first few steps, blood raging through my veins as terror enveloped me.

"Wait," I said weakly. "Did you say, the Abyss?"

Maybe I didn't get out enough, but I didn't think there were any positive connotations to that word. "Um, that doesn't sound good."

Unfortunately, for me and my rampant terror, they all ignored me and kept climbing. I finally had to give up and run after them.

Into the Abyss. Seemingly.

Wicked evaded my frantic attempts to grab him at the top of the steps, running off after Madeline as she disappeared down a long hallway.

A long, long hallway.

I mean a really long, long hallway...

Clearly, we weren't in the Quilleran castle. But I had to wonder at the fact that their house looked just like the...um, entrance to the abyss.

Seemed fitting somehow.

We walked for fifteen minutes, passing the same doors, the same occasional table, the same paintings on the same walls. We'd been going so long I started to worry about the old guy with the walking stick. "How long is this hallway?" I finally asked Madeline.

Her response was a long-suffering smile. As if I were a bratty toddler she was stuck babysitting on a rainy day.

I resembled that statement. After all, I'd spent a *lot* of rainy days stuck inside Croakies with Sebille.

Somewhere along the line, our strides gained a rhythm that I hadn't consciously adopted. I watched Madeline walk, and my strides matched hers. In front of her, the old man's shorter strides mapped to Madeline's. Even Wicked put his feet down in the same rhythm as ours.

Then I noticed a subtle movement where the floor met the walls, and I realized, it wasn't that we kept walking past yard after yard of the same stinkin' walls. It was that the floor was moving while the wall stayed put.

We were on the equivalent of a magical treadmill.

And I was starting to feel like a hamster on a wheel.

To calm my nerves, I decided to ask a lot of annoying questions. "So why does this place look like the Quilleran castle?"

Madeline scanned me a quick look. "Because that's where it is."

I frowned. "Then where is everybody?"

"On their plane."

Before I could stop myself, I glanced upward, as if I could see an airplane flying overhead, filled with Quillerans.

Madeline saw my gaze lift and laughed softly. "Plane as in dimension. When I scryed, I changed the dimension of our destination. Our home dimension doesn't have a portal to the Universe."

"Why does the access point look like the Quilleran castle?"

"It doesn't really. But making it look familiar helps us orient ourselves."

"You could have made it look like your house," I pointed out, channeling my inner, annoying Sebille. "Or Croakies. I'd have felt better about that."

The witch shook her head, frowning. She fell into silence and refused to answer my next three questions, which ran something along the lines of, "Are we there yet? Are we there yet? I have to pee!"

An hour later, I lost my temper. "Madeline!" I barked out, my last nerve becoming my proverbial final straw. "When in a gargoyle's Sunday sneakers are we getting out of this hallway? And when are we going to arrive wherever it is we're going?"

To my surprise, Madeline's gaze snapped to the old man. "I believe we're here."

He jerked to a stop and turned, staring at the same picture we'd passed a hundred times as if it told him something new. It was a large, framed depiction of a bunch of clouds with a gray-blue sky behind them and a strange orange glow sifting through from one corner. "Oh, my. You're correct. Sorry, I was woolgathering."

I felt my lips curl. "I've got some wool you can gather," I mumbled crankily.

The old man reached out with his walking stick and tapped the painting. There was a soft whirring sound, and then the frame clicked and started to fold back, disappearing into the wall as a gust of warm, moist air sifted toward us from the painting.

I felt my eyes go wide as the clouds moved past us, sending a moist haze into the hallway and filling my nose with the scent of ozone.

"You'll have twenty-four hours before the storm hits," the old man said. "See that you're back by then."

"Or what?" I couldn't help asking.

He fixed a slightly hostile gaze on me. "Or you'll be forever part of the Universe."

Yeah, I really didn't like the sound of that.

Madeline stepped through the painting into the clouds. I watched her carefully, expecting her to plunge to her death as she placed her foot onto the fluffy white mass.

She walked on as Rasputin flew through behind her.

Movement near the floor brought my gaze downward, where I found Wicked staring through the opening. He glanced back at me, his gaze narrowing in question. "I don't know, buddy. I think we need to go."

He trotted back to me, stretching up on his hind legs and pawing at my thigh. I lifted him into my arms and moved toward the painting.

A clicking sound made me hesitate as I wavered in the opening.

The old man stepped up behind me. "Hurry up, gal. This portal's about to close."

I half turned, "Close?"

He gave me a grim smile and reached out with his stick, jamming me right between the shoulder blades. "Good luck to ya on your journey, gal."

I stumbled forward, my foot stepping down onto nothing, and I screamed long and hard as we plunged downward, moist white mists hitting me in the face as we fell. My throat raw from screaming, I clutched Wicked so hard I heard his unhappy yowl beneath my screams. I tumbled downward, head over heels, screeching and caterwauling as the clouds and sky lifted away above my head.

Far below me, a quaint scene of rolling green hills dotted with picturesque structures was bounded on all sides by white-topped mountains. It was pretty and somehow familiar. I had a bird's eye view of the pretty place, wherever it was. Except birds didn't plunge straight down toward the ground and splat into those quaint little buildings like we were about to do.

The small town directly below us consisted of crisscrossed ribbons of road with charming little buildings on either side. The structures were colorful and charming in the patchwork view from above. At the center of the village was a pretty white, octangular roof that looked a lot like the gazebo pavilion in the center of Enchanted Park.

I suddenly wished it *was* Enchanted Park. If I was about to die, I would have liked having my beautiful little town be the last thing I saw before I went.

I finally tired of screaming and forced myself to relax and stop clutching Wicked so hard. If we were going to die, screaming wouldn't help. My kitten relaxed in my arms too. My gaze caught on a recognizable shape and I blinked. I'd never seen it from the air before, but there was no mistaking the familiar shape of the place, nor the shaded extension of it that represented the magic enlarging spell.

Still, I wasn't completely sure of the little burg's identity until I saw the giant, clear roof of the greenhouse in the lot behind it.

I was back in Enchanted!

Or, rather, I was about to smash myself into smithereens there.

Not exactly the homecoming I'd hoped for.

13

ENCHANTED DEUX

The ground flew up as I clutched my cat. To my shock, Wicked was purring loudly, his tail beating a happy staccato on the air behind him. I was glad at least that my cat would die with a happy thought on his mind.

We were headed for an unhappy landing on the sidewalk in front of Croakies.

Irony was so very cruel.

I closed my eyes, wishing I'd done more stuff that I'd wanted to do. Unfortunately, all the wonderful moments of my life didn't flash in front of my eyes as they should have. I really wished they had. It would have been fun to relive some of them.

Like the sweet, life-changing moment Maude Quilleran settled Mr. Wicked, fat and fuzzy, into my arms as a kitten...

My uncontrolled downward plummet stopped.

My gaze snapped open, and I was lying face down about ten feet from the surface of the sidewalk. I blinked for a moment, wondering when the final painful drop would crash me into the stained concrete.

Then I slowly rolled upright, and my feet settled gently down onto the ground.

I took a slow, deep breath, willing my heart to stop hammering in my chest and my pulse to slow.

I'd survived!

The door to Croakies opened and the bell jangled. The familiar sound made my chest ache in a totally different way. I realized in that moment that I loved the bookstore, and I loved my life as an artifact keeper. I mean, I got to play with magical toys every day. Who wouldn't love that? Even though some of them tried to eat me. Or stomp me into keeper dust. Or blow snot on me and then pummel me about the head and shoulders with a dismembered gargoyle foot. Yeah, long story for another time.

An elderly woman with a smooth cap of shiny white hair held the door for me, smiling widely. She had an armful of cozy cat mystery books and a mystery lover's gleam in her eyes. "Beautiful day," she said with obvious contentment.

I took another deep breath, smelling the sweetness of my favorite town in all the world, and placed my hand on the door. "It is, isn't it? Thanks so much."

"That's an adorable little baby you have there," she said, giving Wicked a scratch under the chin.

I nodded, watching her walk down the street. She reminded me a lot of Mrs. Foxladle, and that thought made me smile.

"Are ya gonna just stand there all day lettin' the flies in?" called a raspy, decidedly male voice from inside Croakies. Stepping through the door, I let it slide closed behind me. I stood looking around, not sure if I was seeing correctly.

The store looked like Croakies. But it didn't look like *my* Croakies.

"Can I help you find something?"

I glanced toward the unfamiliar voice, frowning when I saw the short, balding round man crouched behind the counter, eyeing me like Mr. Slimy eyed his next meal on wings.

I glanced back toward the door. Beyond the glass of the front window, the ugly wooden Croakies sign trembled on the end of its chains from a soft breeze. The unattractive spotted frog looked less worn than I remembered, but it was definitely my sign. "I'm..."

At a loss for what to say, I turned back to the bulgy-eyed man standing at my counter. "I'm Naida Griffith."

He held my gaze a beat longer and then came out from behind the counter, moving across the shop on bowed legs and out-turned feet that reminded me of Mr. Slimy's. He extended a small, pudgy hand. "Nice to meet you, Naida. What are you selling today? I'm afraid I'm up to my eyebrows in bookmarks. But I could use a few more book lights if you have some of those. My customers just can't seem to get enough of them."

My lips flapped unattractively. "Your...customers?"

He narrowed the bulgy brown eyes on me. "Are you okay? You look a little pale." His gaze slid to Wicked, who'd been uncharacteristically still since we'd entered the store. I'd expected him to struggle to get down and explore. The man grimaced. "Cats aren't allowed in here."

I gave up the attempt to keep my mouth closed on that one. "But...Mr. Wicked lives here."

"Not in my store, he doesn't," the man said adamantly. "Frogs and cats don't get along."

"Frogs?"

He pointed to a large terrarium on the back wall. The enormous container took up the space where I kept my small bookshelves filled with children's magical books. The spotless glass box was filled with all sizes, shapes and colors of frogs.

My gaze slid from the terrarium to the waving sign outside.

He chuckled, apparently seeing me make the connection. "Yep. That's where the name of the store came from." His sour expression softened when he talked about his frogs. He clearly loved them like I loved my cat. "I should introduce myself," he suddenly said, grinning. "Bandy Joe Barrows. I own this sweet little shop."

My knees just about gave out on me. Bandy Joe had been the first owner of Croakies. An ancient, and by all accounts, powerful sorcerer whose familiar of choice had been a frog.

How was it possible I was standing there speaking to him?

Where the heck had the Universe belched me out?

"Are you sure you're okay," Bandy Joe asked, his frog-like gaze locked onto my face. I'd felt all the blood leaving my cheeks so I could guess how pale I looked. What did I do? Bandy Joe didn't seem to know who I was so I could assume the Universe hadn't put me at Croakies for some pre-arranged purpose. But I was there for a reason. Even if neither Croakies' original owner nor I knew what it was.

I frowned.

He stared at me and swallowed, his fleshy throat bulging slightly with the movement.

Surely there was a reason I'd been flung into the current reality. It couldn't have been a mistake...

Wait...

Shirley.

I gave Bandy Joe a smile. "You might not understand this but..." I looked toward the ceiling and tugged on the familiar thread of my keeper magic.

Her name was a question on my mind. "Shirley? I'm talking to you."

The air erupted in sparks above our heads and I flinched away from them, watching Bandy Joe's expression and waiting.

He didn't look all that surprised.

There was a burst of light, and a tiny creature with dirty-blonde pin curls all over her head hung in the air in front of us, her dark-blonde eyebrows slashing judgment across her face. The Pixie's enormous moth-like wings undulated rhythmically behind her.

The supernormal world's version of a Witch-a-pedia glared down on me, crossing her tiny arms over her chest after flinging a less intense glare in the other keeper's direction.

"Hey, Joe," she inexplicably said.

"Hi, Shirley."

She pursed her lips at his use of her common name but didn't correct him as she always corrected me. "What is your question?" she ground out in my direction.

The Pixie was the supernormal world's go-to source for fun trivia and occasionally useful information about all magical families and their ancestors. Unfortunately, she hated her job. Being the Witch-a-pedia for everyone else seemed to grate on her nerves.

Which, I suspected, was the reason she never wanted anyone to call her.

"Hey, Shirley."

She cocked a hip and glared at me. "I told you not to call me that."

"I need to know the reason for my being here."

She glanced at Bandy Joe again, her drab brown wings slowly beating the air above my head. To my shock, he inclined his head as if giving her permission to speak.

Shirley huffed out an irritated breath. "You're here because the Universe wants you here."

I shook my head as she started to glow, readying for departure. "Not yet, Shirley. I need to know *why* the Universe wants me here."

She looked at Joe again, and my last nerve twanged. "Stop looking at him, Shirrrrleeey," I said, drawing out her name just to irritate her. "I'm the one who called you. Not him."

"She can't answer because she doesn't know," Joe said, narrowing his froggy eyes at me.

Shirley's cheeks turned pink. She might not like being the Witch-a-pedia Supernormal, but, apparently, she also didn't like when she didn't know something.

"Don't call me again." She disappeared in a burst of light that left behind a slight sulfur stench.

I turned to Joe. "You know who I am?"

He held my gaze for a moment and then nodded. "The order came through a few minutes ago."

"Then why didn't you say anything?"

He shrugged. "It's not my place. This is your journey. It's up to you to determine how you want to take it."

That just wasn't helpful at all. "Well, I'm in trouble then, because I don't have a clue."

He nodded, scrubbing a hand over his chin. "I thought so. Okay, first of all, I sense a frog in your life."

I nodded and he grinned. "Mr. Sl..." I hesitated, instinctively knowing that the frog-loving keeper would be offended by the name. "Um, I call him Mr. Rustin."

Bandy Joe's grin widened. "A very superior name. I'm guessing then, that you know what excellent magic conductors frogs are?"

"Um...Yes?" I did know they came in handy for unscrupulous witches to stick unwitting souls into.

He nodded. "Good. Then, let's get to work."

I followed him over to the terrarium, my palms growing sweaty as I realized he was going to extract one of the frogs from the container. He reached inside and pulled out a fat, spotted guy who was about the same size as Lea's burly bullfrog. "This guy here excels in conducting the emotional magics. His transference style is very mellow and gives one a smooth, predictable outcome." He replaced the fat one in the glass container and plucked a cute little light green one with bright red eyes off a tree branch. "This tree frog is very good for avarice issues. He changes color when confronted with unbridled avarice." He settled the tree frog back onto its branch and pulled out a long, narrow frog with eyes that fixed on my face with the intensity of a priest trying to read my soul. "This little guy judges intent. You won't fool him," Bandy Joe happily announced as I squirmed.

He held the little frog against his chest, petting him like a puppy, and beamed over at me. "So which one will it be?"

I thought over my choices, wondering what the other frogs in the terrarium were good for and why he hadn't broken them out for me to choose.

I chewed my lip with indecision.

Wicked shoved out of my grasp as I was trying to decide and bounced toward his favorite corner, probably hoping to catch a bit of string or fluff unaware.

I sighed. "I just don't know. Probably avarice. But I don't actually know what I'm dealing with."

"Tell me about the artifact."

I filled him in on the gold coin creating purse and the humans who'd suffered under its poisonous appeal.

When I was done, Joe frowned. He settled the narrow frog into the bottom of the glass container and reached both hands behind a large rock, pulling out a frog that looked to be as big as my head. He held the enormous thing up to me. "Corruption. It sounds to me as if we're dealing with corrupt Powers That Be."

I glanced around, waiting for a lightning bolt to zap him for saying that out loud. He must have noticed because he chuckled. "Don't worry. They aren't omnipotent. But they are too powerful some-times for their own good."

"You think a PTB gave the artifact to the Yens?" He nodded. "But why?"

"Well, first of all, the order came from the Universe, not the local PTB. That tells me there's something rotten in the Cosmos that going to the local PTB won't fix. Secondly, PTB aren't allowed to benefit from the artifacts they create. It's a cardinal rule. Breaking that rule is punished by instant oblit-eration, floating through the Universe for the rest of their shattered existence in tiny little pieces which carry the muscle memory of that pain and keep it alive."

I grimaced.

He nodded. "Yes, it's brutal. It's meant to be. You can imagine what would happen if all PTB were able to create artifacts and then use them willy-nilly for self-gain."

I certainly could. "Okay, I get that. But how does that help us? Why would they give the Yens something that poisoned them? That wouldn't help the PTB at all."

"Two possibilities come to mind, Naida keeper. First, if the PTB had a connection to the magical world who could make use of the artifact, indirectly helping them both, the rule might not be, technically, considered broken."

"So I might be looking for a relative or friend of a PTB?"

"Yes."

I thought of Madeline Quilleran. She certainly had relatives galore who'd love to thwart the Universe for their own gain.

"And secondly, this could simply be the result of rage or jealousy. Even the PTB are capable of both."

"I don't understand."

He nodded. "Assume you're PTB and you see lesser magic users or, even more irritating, non-magic humans making use of magical artifacts every day, yet you're denied the same benefits those lesser, according to the PTB's jaded way of looking at things, creatures have access to. Don't you suppose that might grate a bit after a few centuries?"

I certainly did suppose it. "That makes sense. So, what you're telling me is that I'm either looking for someone who wants untold riches or someone who's mad at the world and looking to punish those he or she thinks deserve punishment."

He nodded. "That's about the gist of it."

I thought about his ideas for a moment and then sighed. "Okay, that makes perfect sense, but there's probably no end of people out there who fit both possibilities. How do I figure out which ones I'm looking for?"

Bandy Joe nodded, replacing the ten-pound corruption frog into the terrarium. "We utilize a witch, of course."

14

CORRUPTION AND GREED WALK INTO A BAR...

I wasn't surprised to discover Lea next door. Not really. But I was a little surprised that she looked so different in the current dimension. Unlike, Bandy Joe, who'd apparently been warned I was coming, she didn't have a clue who I was.

My friend came through the front door of Croakies wearing a navy business suit with a high-necked white blouse. Her wavy, light brown hair was cut into a chin-length bob, and her turquoise gaze was serious.

She smiled when Bandy Joe introduced us, pumping my hand like a politician. "It's a pleasure to meet you, Naida. I didn't think there was ever more than one keeper of the artifacts." She looked a question toward Joe.

He shook his head. "Within each dimension, that's true. Naida comes from another plane."

Lea's eyes widened with interest. "Wow, chilled."

Okay, some things didn't change. Lea still couldn't get current slang right.

"I have a Leandra in my dimension too," I told her.

"Really? What's she like?"

"Probably a lot like you. Except she's more of a flower child, really."

Lea laughed. "The real me then." She glanced toward Joe. "What's up? You needed my help with something?"

He nodded toward me. "Give her the rundown on what's happening."

I told her about my situation at home. About traveling to their dimension with Madeline Quilleran...

"Wait," she stopped me, mid-explanation. "You came with Madeline? Why?"

"She's a PTB, and she's helping me find out who's behind the artifact leakages."

"Then where is she?" Lea asked, quite reasonably.

I blinked, immediately seeing her point. "Um. I guess I just assumed we got separated when we entered the Universe."

"You entered together?" Lea's gaze slid to Joe's.

"Well, yeah." I frowned. "But she didn't drop into this dimension when we came through the door."

Lea's gaze sharpened. "Drop? What do you mean? Did you see where she went?"

I shook my head. "No. She hit the clouds and walked across them. When I stepped through the door, I fell like a rock to this place. It wasn't my favorite way to travel, let me tell you."

"Fascinating." She looked again to Joe. "Did you know about this dimension-hopping?"

"Only that it was possible."

"Are the PTB the same across dimensions?" I asked him.

"Yes. The Universe and the PTB are the same." He frowned. "But the system is based on certain iron-clad rules."

"Like what?" Lea asked.

"Well, for one, PTBs never cross dimensions. It's not allowed. Keeping them widely separated protects the ruling body from those who might try to undermine or destroy it. That way, only one PTB can be compromised at a time."

"Then how did she...?" I started to ask.

"She used Naida to cross." Lea murmured over me. "Diabolical."

Joe nodded. "Which begs the question. Why?"

"Why did she cross?" Lea said, nodding. "And what is she up to?"

"And why am I *here*?" I asked. "In this particular dimension?"

Joe and Lea looked startled. Finally, Lea nodded. "You came to the Universe with a particular need. It sounds like they selected you to fix whatever breach has occurred. So we have to assume that the core of the problem is here."

"If that's true, why didn't Madeline come here too?" I asked.

Joe fixed his protuberant brown gaze on me, his lips tightening. "Because she's not here to help you, Naida keeper. Madeline Quilleran has her own agenda."

"Gargoyle sneakers," I muttered. "That can't be good."

Joe bounced on his out-turned feet as if he would start hopping. Wringing his hands together, he glanced toward the door. "We should start. I'll close the store."

Lea nodded. "Which frogs did we decide on?"

Joe locked the front entrance, waving his hands slowly over the physical deadbolts until the warding snicked into place with a puff of black smoke. "Corruption and greed, I think. We'll rule those out and then move on if necessary."

Wicked came bouncing over from the other side of the store, weaving around Lea's ankles with a loud purr.

She looked down and smiled. "Well, hello, handsome boy. You look just like my sweet Hex."

I smiled. "You have a Hex here? There's one at home too."

"What's his name?"

"Mr. Wicked. In my world..." It felt so strange saying that. "Wicked and Hex are from the same litter."

"Then there should be a Wicked here too," She said. "Things always match up."

"Not everything apparently." I pointed toward Joe. "There's no me here."

"Hm, yeah, you're right," Lea said, frowning. "I wonder why?"

I did too. But her statement was bothering me. What if the Quillerans still had Wicked in this dimension. "Where did you get Hex?" I asked Lea.

"From a young witch."

"Maude Quilleran?"

She nodded. "What's wrong? You look upset."

"If it's like at home, there's a whole litter of kittens. The Quillerans are using them for bad things. We need to find them."

Lea nodded. "Just tell me where they are. Queen Sindy and I will find them and get them to a safe place."

Relieved, I gave her a quick rundown of the situation with Wicked's littermates. I'd recently had to clean that mess up at home and couldn't bear the thought of those sweet kittens being stuck with the nasty Quilleran witches.

"Ready?" Joe asked, his cheeks puffing with excitement. The longer I was around the other artifact keeper, the more he looked like the frogs he preferred.

We headed toward the connecting door. Mr. Wicked bounded happily ahead.

I looked at Lea, asking the question I'd been dying to ask since figuring out where I was. "Is there a Princess Sebille here?"

Lea grimaced. "Foul creature. She gives Queen Sindy fits."

"Does she live in Toadstool City then?"

Lea nodded. "Though every chance she gets, she busts out and gets big. That's one rebellious Sprite, let me tell you."

I chuckled. "You have no idea."

Corruption and greed walked into a bar... oh...wait...that's another story. In *this* story, they squatted in the center of a protective circle, surrounded by well-used white candles whose flames flickered from green to red to orange as Lea sifted dust over them.

I thought she was using a type of fairy dust, but I

didn't want to ask while she was in the middle of her spell.

Joe and I stood off to the side, watching. His attention was fixed firmly on the proceedings at the center of the artifact library, but mine was continually drawn around the space, assessing the artifacts Joe was managing.

None of them looked familiar. I finally turned to him. "My artifacts are totally different from yours."

He nodded. "That actually makes perfect sense. None of us could possibly house all the artifacts in the Universe."

"True." My gaze kept getting locked on a metal box sitting on a worktable nearby. "What does that one do?"

Joe slid the box a quick look. "I'm not sure, exactly. That just came into my possession last week. I haven't had time to put it through its paces. As far as I can tell, it's a fully developed miniature world." He grinned. "Check this out." I walked with him to the table, and he tugged the box closer. "See that window there?"

I nodded.

"Watch this." He stuck his finger through the window and, after a beat, it disappeared.

My eyes went wide. "Where'd it go?"

"It's still there, look closely."

I leaned down and narrowed my gaze, seeing a

teeny-tiny protuberance on his hand where the finger had been.

Joe pulled his finger back out, and the digit regained its normal dimensions.

"Awesome sauce!" I said with a chuckle.

Joe laughed too. "I love my job."

Across the room, Lea cleared her throat and Joe and I flinched, turning to the irritated witch giving us the evil eye. "Do you two think you could focus long enough to help me with this spell?"

Mumbling our apologies, Joe and I hurried back to the circle.

Lea had all the candles dusted. The flames were a foot high on each one and flashed a beautiful rainbow of colors around the two frogs.

My gaze scanned past the two frogs and then stopped, reversing in horror. Corruption had grown to the size of a small cat. I thought Greed might have grown a bit too, but nothing like his rotund friend. "What does that mean?" I asked Lea.

She frowned. "We won't know for sure until I use the data in my scrying, but just off the top of my head I'm guessing corruption is close."

"Isn't it always?" Joe murmured, making me grin.

Lea pointed to a spot on the circle that would be between about seven and eight on a clock. "Naida, I need you to stand there." She pointed to the corresponding spot on the other side, breaking the circle up into rough thirds. "Joe, you stand there."

We got into position, and Lea pulled a container of something green from her bag. Reaching inside, she grabbed a handful of the dry dust.

"Do you scry with Mercury?" I asked the witch.

My Lea scryed with Mercury, so I assumed the current Lea would too.

"No. I'm an herbal witch. I scry with herbs."

Hm, I'd have to share that with *my* Lea. She was an herbal witch too.

"I used to utilize Mercury," she told me as she took a handful of the herbs and threw them into the air above the circle. The herbal dust filtered out into the shape of a dome whose edges were the exact perimeter of the circle, as if the line on the floor Lea had made with herbs rather than salt formed a barrier the dust couldn't pass. As the herbs hit the boundary, they started to rotate, the dust in the center dipping and rising as Lea worked a spell with her fingers on the air.

I watched in fascination as she worked. It never ceased to amaze me what witches could do. Their magic was so complex and multi-layered. In fact, that was the aspect that separated sorceresses like me from witches like Lea. Sorceresses generally only had access to one type of magic. Our legacy magic. Legacy magic tied closely to the jobs we were destined to perform during our lifetimes. Though some of us learned to manipulate other types of energy during our existence, we were really only good at one thing. In my case, it was managing and using magical artifacts.

Though I'd be the first to admit I wasn't fully trained in the job yet. The keeper of the artifacts who'd trained me had been more interested in moving on to her next great adventure than in helping me figure out mine.

I returned my attention to Lea's scrying. The surface of the dome had flattened out, leaving a variety of elevations and shapes above the plane of the whole. From the side, it looked like a small cityscape I didn't recognize. But when Lea sliced her hand across the spell she'd written on the air, the strands of magic were severed. They retracted into the scrying surface. Slowly, the entire thing dropped to the floor, hovering for a moment over the two frogs, and then spinning a quarter of a cycle and dropping to the floor.

I suddenly realized that I was looking at a topographic representation of Enchanted. And each of the frogs was situated in one of the places on the map.

Lea pointed to Corruption. "I'd say that's where your culprit is."

I walked around the circle and eyed the layout carefully. I knew exactly where that was. "Do you have giants in the city?" I asked.

Lea looked at Joe, frowning. "Not that I know of. Joe?"

He shook his head. "No giants. I'd know if we did. Why?"

I stared at the two-story-tall brick building, seeing it in my mind's eye as Enchanted Collateral. "Because, at home, that's a pawn shop owned by a giant."

"If the culprit is in this dimension as we think he is, your giant is off the hook for this, Naida keeper," Joe said.

Relief flooded me. I hadn't wanted Theo to be guilty. "Then what *is* located there?"

"I don't know," Lea said, shrugging. "Let's go see."

15

BUGGED

The building looked like Enchanted Collateral. But it wasn't. And I wasn't quite sure how corruption fit into the business I was looking at. Not directly. Though, I could definitely see greed being a factor.

"It's a bank?" Joe frowned. "That's weird."

Instead of the pawnshop sign I was used to seeing, there was a carved stone placard bearing a depiction of a dragon breathing fire and the inscription, "Dragon Savings and Loan".

"Maybe somebody's getting special treatment from the loan officer."

I shook my head. "Did you see the size of that frog?"

Lea nodded. "You're right. There's something much bigger going on here."

"It has to be tied to a person rather than the business," Joe offered.

That made as much sense as anything, I supposed. "Let's go inside and ask for the bank manager."

We'd start at the top and work our way through the employees.

The lobby was mostly empty when we stepped inside. One young mother was filling out a deposit slip at the wooden kiosk in the center of the space. Her young toddler clung to her leg, watching us through enormous blue eyes filled with curiosity.

The woman behind the long counter eyed us with suspicion as we came inside. I wasn't sure if we looked shifty, or if it was the fact that I was carrying a very annoyed gray cat in my arms.

Wicked wanted to jump down and snoop around. I was tempted to let him. He'd shown better instincts so far than I had for finding magical trouble.

"What can we do for you today?" the woman asked, giving us an insincere smile.

I walked toward the counter. "We'd like to speak to the bank manager."

The woman frowned, throwing a glance toward an office near the back of the lobby. The door was closed, but I could see a brass sign on its surface that said, *Manager*. The office had large windows that overlooked the lobby. Shades had been drawn over them on the inside.

"It's really important," Lea said, leaning close to the woman with a smile. "We'd be very grateful if you'd let him know we're here." She touched the woman's hand as she spoke to her. A soft green glow flared briefly to life and then disappeared. As Lea pulled away, a smidgen of green dust fell to the counter and dissipated with a hiss.

Lea winked at me and I bit my lip to keep from smiling.

The doubt in the clerk's gaze smoothed away and she smiled. "Of course. I'll be right back." She pushed through the swinging door in the counter and strode forward with a stiff gate and a blank gaze. She was moving as if under some kind of impulsion.

Joe started after her. "Come on," he said in a low tone of voice.

The woman knocked twice and then opened the door to stick her head inside without waiting for a response. "There are people here to see you."

The man behind the desk frowned, his small face unhappy beneath a spiky spray of coal-black hair. He fixed an almond-shaped brown gaze on the clerk and clenched his small fist. "I'm in the middle of a meeting..."

Joe pushed the door open and stepped past the woman, his bowed legs eating up the distance between the door and the woman sitting regally in a chair across from him. "Hello Madeline," he said as we stepped past the poor, befuddled clerk. "Fancy meeting you here."

I gasped in surprise. "Madeline, where have you been?"

The raven on her shoulder flapped his wings in irritation, but Madeline Quilleran touched his foot as if to shush him. Her smile for me appeared genuine. "There you are, dear. We've been looking all over for you."

I slid my gaze to the disgruntled young bank manager. "Yeah, because obviously I'd be in a bank."

Madeline's lips thinned. "Don't be silly. Fu and I are old friends. I simply stopped by to see him."

Joe had been studying the manager since we came into the room. He narrowed his froggy gaze. "Old friends, huh?"

Fu leaned away from Joe, curling his lip as if the keeper carried a deadly, magic-eating virus. "What do you people want?"

"That's not a very welcoming attitude for a bank manager," Lea said, also eying Fu with an intense gaze.

Feeling like I was missing something, I narrowed my gaze on him too.

"Why are you all squinting at me?" he asked.

I didn't know what the others were seeing, but recognition flared for me. "What's your last name, Fu?"

He crossed his arms over his chest, the expensive-looking suit stretching over his narrow shoulders with the movement. "What's *your* name?"

"I'm Naida Griffith," I told him, leaving out the important part.

"She's a KoA," Madeline told him helpfully.

I clenched my teeth with frustration. Had Madeline spilled the beans about my designation just to be helpful? Or was she warning him somehow? Judging by the meaningful gaze they shared, I figured it was the latter.

"Let me make this easy for you," I told the manager. "Your name's Yen, isn't it?"

His face paled. "I want you to leave."

"And you're PTB, aren't you?" Joe said. "I could feel the power pulsing off you as soon as we entered the bank."

Yen jumped to his feet and threw his arms into the air. He screamed something in a language I didn't understand, probably Chinese given his obvious nationality, and jumped into the air. A bright light flashed, and a six-foot-long brown bug with a wide body that looked like it was covered in armor landed on top of the bank manager's desk with a thud.

We all backpedaled as a putrid stench wafted through the room.

"Ew!" I grumbled, covering my nose. "That's just nasty."

Lea's hands were busily writing a spell on the air.

Joe was studying the giant bug Fu Yen had transformed himself into. "Stink bug," he said to no one in particular. "Nasty things. Toxic to frogs." He took a step backward as the disgusting insect threateningly brandished its antennae his way.

Alarm making my chest tight, I glanced around the office for Mr. Wicked. I'd somehow lost my grip on him during the shock of the big, stinky reveal. He was probably hiding under the desk.

Madeline was still sitting in her chair, looking bored.

I wanted to be her when I grew up. That was, if she wasn't completely, irretrievably evil.

The jury was still out on that.

Even Ras was dancing nervously from side to side as the massive insect loomed over them. He settled a worried, beady gaze on Madeline. "Maddie, it seems prudent to give this creature some space."

But Madeline didn't break eye contact with Yen, a slight smile on her lips.

I narrowed my gaze on her and saw the faint motes of magic dancing on the air between them. Were they conversing silently? If so, what were they saying? I didn't think they were contemplating how to be more helpful.

I nudged Bandy Joe with my elbow. "I think they're communicating."

"Huh? Who?"

"The two PTB."

He studied them for a moment and then glanced at Lea. "Can you isolate the bug?"

She nodded, her fingers still dancing on the air. The well-manicured digits were moving so quickly I could barely see them. A series of fine, green lines grew from her fingertips, forming into a series of sigils which I probably should have recognized. Unfortunately, as a student, I'd discovered I could really only concentrate on one subject at a time. Sigils 101 hadn't been nearly as interesting as Magical Leaps and Bounds 101, so...

Which gave me an idea. "Do you want me to leap over the bug a few times?"

Joe and Lea both looked at me, their confusion a nearly physical presence between us.

I flushed, shrugging. "You know, to distract them?"

Lea turned back to her spell-making and Joe rolled his eyes.

Suddenly, I felt as if I were back at Croakies with Sebille. At some point in my future, I was going to have to do some self-assessment exercises to determine why everyone around me was always rolling their eyes.

But not right at that moment.

The stink bug suddenly lifted its back end and tensed. A wave of foul air, like a cloud of mist stained yellow-orange, exploded from its backside.

The wave hit Lea and sent her flying backward to splat against the wall. She slid downward on a slimy wash of orange-tinted goo, her hands held out in front of her and a grimace coloring her face. "Oh, goddess!" she exclaimed, shaking her hands and sending goo flying all round.

Joe recoiled, his face turning green and his throat working as he fell to the ground on all fours.

I stared at him, expecting him to shift into a frog at any moment.

My eyes stung and my nostrils tried to seal themselves closed in self-defense. I staggered through the door into the lobby, sucking in a big gulp of untainted air.

I felt sick. My face burned as if I'd been magically pepper-sprayed.

The bug reared up and shook its nasty antennae at us, wielding them like blades.

I danced back just as one of the things swept past my face, and felt the burning pain of a glancing connection. Apparently, in addition to an extremely disgusting stench, the bug had razors in its antennae too.

I noticed Yen kept his attacks focused on the three of us. Madeline sat very still, her gaze locked on Yen. I couldn't help wondering if she was somehow influencing his behavior.

Lea had climbed back to her feet and was trying to form a fresh spell on the air, but her fingers were still covered with goo, and she didn't seem to be having much luck. "Lea! The witch!" I hoped that instruction was vague enough that Madeline might not catch on if she was distracted, but on-point enough that Lea would understand.

If she was as quick as *my* Lea she'd get it.

She tried to fling another spell at the bug, but it died under a quelling layer of goop.

Joe pulled a small, lined notebook from his pocket. He tugged an old-fashioned quill-type pen out too and began jotting something onto the page.

Seeing Lea's problem, I decided it would be up to me to stop Madeline. I shuddered at the thought but realized it was my fault she was there. And therefore my responsibility. I was taking a step toward the witch when I felt a soft, warmth rubbing against my calf.

I yelped in surprise and looked down to find Wicked sitting on the Book of Pages, his orange gaze narrowing as he purred.

The book! Thank goodness the book seemed drawn to my familiar. Wicked seemed able to call it from wherever it was. Even, apparently, across dimensions.

I reached down and Mr. Wicked jumped off the leather-encased tome as I picked it up. Running my palm over the cover, I gritted my teeth as the leather warmed and rolled beneath my touch.

The book flipped open. Pages started to flash past.

As I tried to come up with something that I could use against the bug, an antenna slashed through the flickering pages, slicing through several sheets and sending the book flying.

I jumped back as pain burned across my palm. Glancing down, I saw the first droplets of blood rising from the wound. A putrid stench rose with the blood. "Ugh!"

Mr. Wicked yowled angrily and leaped onto the desk.

"Wicked, no!" I watched in horror as all the fur on his back lifted and he hissed his rage, slashing a fully-clawed paw across the bug's underbelly.

The nasty creature staggered back with a roar, a fresh stench wafting toward us as the wounds bled a slimy green.. Unfortunately, Yen recovered too quickly, spinning around so fast my vision couldn't register the movement and sending another cloud of nasty goo over Wicked.

He hissed, yowled, and sailed backward into my arms as the blast hit him, taking us both down to the ground.

I watched in horror as the bug jumped down from the desk, heading right for us. "Lea!"

"I'm trying," she screamed back. "This goo is interfering with the magic somehow."

There was a flash of light behind the bug, but

nothing happened. It kept coming, its nasty, buggy face topped by a pair of mean, rust-colored eyes. The tiny feet pattered nastily across the floor, closing the distance between the desk and us in mere seconds.

An antenna ripped past my face. Wicked yowled and jumped at it, giving a chirp of frustration as the goo weighed him down. He missed the bladed antenna by several inches, splatting back down to the carpet beneath us.

Another antenna slashed and I gave a short bark of pain as it left a burning trail along my arm.

Lea appeared behind the thing and threw her hands into the air, emitting a short burst of green powder that fizzled into dust at her feet. "Explode it!" she yelled in frustration.

I winced, figuring she probably meant "blast it!" and had gotten it woefully wrong as usual.

Another slicing antenna had me scrambling for the book as a fresh wound opened up under the torn fabric of my jeans.

I slammed my palm onto the open page and thought about the artifact I knew could combat the blade-like antennae.

Blackbeard's sword appeared in my hand in a silvery burst of light. A second eruption ended in a round of bleeping as a colorful, feathered dust ball rolled through the air and smacked into the gigantic bug.

"Bloody bleep!" SB squawked, finally finding his

wings and taking off just as an antenna slashed in his direction. "What fresh bleep hath ye wrought, Lass?"

SB circled the room and landed on my shoulder as I climbed to my feet, the sword already dancing in my hand.

"Just keep him busy, Naida," Lea told me. "I've almost got this." A green cloud of magic exploded from her fingertips, flared outward as if it might catch hold, and then shriveled and dusted the carpet near her sensible business pumps. Lea let lose a twisted swear, which fell flat along with the dust.

I danced lightly on my toes, leading the bug toward the door. Eyeing the bug's wide, armored body, I'd had an idea. If I could get him to wedge himself into the too-narrow door, I might be able to contain him until Lea got her magic to work.

"'Tis certain ye might be that ye've bested Blackbeard's blade," SB intoned from my shoulder as the bug advanced and I slashed with the sword, leaving a bloody trail alongside the already healing tracks of Wicked's claws. "But rest assured ye've met yer match, and ye'll soon be dancin' with the dead."

A little dramatic, but apparently enough to annoy the bug into following as I backstepped toward the door.

An antenna shot toward SB. He lifted smoothly off my shoulder as it sliced past. Though the burning pain in my cheek told me I hadn't been so lucky.

Without thinking, I swung the sword again, opening up a vertical slash the length of Yen's buggy form.

Rather than slowing it down, the attacks seemed to drive the monster forward, his answering strike so swift and violent that it sent me stumbling backward. My heel caught on the threshold of the door and I went down on my back. SB launched himself into the air on an outraged squawk.

Unfortunately, the bug didn't follow me through the door. It stopped just inside, whipping around before I could scramble away, and sending another wave of goo over me and the unfortunate parrot.

The weight of the stuff carried me to the floor, flat on my back. The sword fell from my hands, suddenly feeling like a boulder in my hand, and SB dropped like a chunk of feathered, foul-mouthed lead to the ground, smacking hard into my shoulder.

I lay there a long moment, so overcome by the weight and stench of the goo that I couldn't move.

I was vaguely aware of footsteps and screaming behind me. Most of the pounding footsteps were heading away, through the exterior door I heard repeatedly slamming closed. One set came toward me.

They stopped nearby, and a familiar round face with bulging brown eyes peered down at me. "Are you all right?" Bandy Joe asked, two lines of concern appearing between his froggy eyes.

I tried to nod but my head wouldn't move. "I can't do much but I'm fine."

He nodded. "We've got this." He hurried toward the office, where the bug had turned away and was menacing something out of sight. I assumed it was Lea since it didn't seem interested in going after Madeline.

I glared at the Quilleran witch as the bug cleared the doorway, leaving me with a line of sight to her. She sat unmoving as before, her gaze straight ahead, and it struck me that her actions, or lack thereof, were strange and unnatural. Something was going on there that I couldn't see.

Almost as if reading my mind, Rasputin rose up from her shoulder and flew toward me. He landed on a nearby desk and glared down at SB and me.

The parrot was on his feet again but he only seemed able to walk in circles, his gaze filled with confusion. Goo pressed his feathers flat and made his wings droop uselessly at his sides.

"A fine mess you've made of things, Naida keeper." Rasputin sneered.

"Shut it, you!" I grumbled. "A little help would be nice."

He cocked his sleek black head. "What do you think Maddie's doing, sorceress?"

I managed to shove to my knees, but it felt as if I was wearing a weighted blanket. "As far as I can see, nothing helpful."

The bird made a disgusted whistling sound. "If she hadn't put a magical padlock on him, he'd have been gone a long time ago. But that type of magic is very difficult. It requires supreme concentration. She wanted me to tell you that you can subdue him any time now. She has things she needs to do."

I pushed to my feet, groaning. "Yeah, we'll talk about *that* later. She shouldn't even be here," I told the bird, stabbing a goo-coated finger at him. The raven rose up off the desk with an appalled squawk as a heavy droplet of gunk landed in the spot where he'd been. "Watch it, girl! That stuff's nasty."

"Really?" I asked him, using my best Sebille imitation. "I hadn't noticed."

"Don't forget *me*, Lass," SB said, waddling around like a slimy arctic penguin.

I felt a helpless grin forming at the sight. "You're looking a little bottom-heavy there, SB."

If birds could only glower... "Har de har," he said. "Pick me up ye wee, blackguard. Or I'll poop in yer cornflakes on the morrow."

I bit back a response, not wanting to push him too far. I wouldn't put it past him to make good on his threat.

"I can't believe you lot can't best one bug," Rasputin sneered again.

I tried to put SB on my shoulder but he kept sliding off, so I grabbed him back, holding him like a chicken in my arms.

At Rasputin's nasty razzing, the parrot and I shared a look.

SB nodded. "Do what ye must, Lass."

"Are you sure?"

"Aye. The cur has it comin' to 'im."

I turned around and gave Rasputin a look. "Humility is a virtue, bird. And kindness is a golden light in your soul."

The raven snorted as I'd known he would. So I flung the parrot in his direction, hoping I'd gotten the height and distance right.

SB fought his wings to pound the air heavily a couple of times, giving him the additional couple of inches I'd miscalculated, and then slammed into the raven before Rasputin had time to do more than squawk. The two of them hit the surface of the unmanned desk and skidded across its shiny surface, toppling backward off the desk and landing with a thwuck on the desk chair.

I trudged heavily past, glancing over to make sure SB was okay.

I grinned. He was more than okay. He was happily rolling around on the raven, transferring some of his goo onto the snotty, arrogant creature as Rasputin squawked and swore and generally had a hissy fit.

"Ye bilge-sucking dog of a wicked mum, whose pride for ye be small, ye'll succumb to Blackbeard's mighty bird, 'fore yer mum's tears of shame can fall."

I chuckled, shuffling toward the stinky bug problem in the manager's office.

Usually pretentiously precise and arrogantly verbose, Rasputin had been reduced to squawks and swears under the prodigious force of the gunk-drenched parrot and his slimy goo.

I couldn't help thinking that, despite its challenges, the day was turning out to have its high points.

16

PULL YE TOES FROM THE GANGPLANK

a stinky blast of noxious goop flew through the door and glopped onto the short carpet inches in front of me.

I eased to the side, letting the wall protect me as I peered into the room.

Lea stood near the back wall, dripping with what looked like a fresh layer of smelly goop.

She held her hands behind her, probably trying to protect them from a new layer of the magic-sapping stuff.

Bandy Joe was covered in slime too, his short, muscular body dripping with the stuff and a puddle of it glistening around his feet. I was surprised to see that he was holding the metal box from Croakies. I had no idea how he'd gotten hold of it, but I did have some idea what he wanted to use it for.

He glanced at me as I peeked through the door.

"A little help here," he growled out, gunk sliding down his round face.

"What do you want me to do?"

"Distract the bug again so I can give him the load of energy I have here," Lea said, her eyes going wide as the bug spun around, clearly intending to dose her again. "Fast!" she screamed.

I turned to look at the sword. It was too far away, especially with my heavy coating of slime. It would take me a few minutes to shuffle out there and shamble back with it. And swinging it would probably prove impossible.

What else...? My gaze slid to Madeline. *Did I dare?*

"Beware the blackguard!" SB screeched out behind me. I spun to find a very unsteady Rasputin flying...if you could call it that...right toward me.

He pounded his wings like a bloated ostrich trying to take off, sending slime drops everywhere as he fought the weight to try to stay aloft.

I ducked to the side, knowing a perfect opportunity when I spotted it. I stuck my head through the door. "Incoming!" The big bird flew clumsily past and, as he cleared the door, I gave him a shove, adding a wisp of keeper magic for good measure, and sent him flying out of control and at a speed he couldn't have achieved on his own with a dense coating of bug glop.

Rasputin gave his wings another desperate

thrust as he started to lose altitude and then looked up to find himself steering too close to his target. He tried to pull up, his wings flung out to the side and his body going nearly vertical in an attempt to keep from smashing into his destination.

But it was no good.

He couldn't stop.

With a final, terrified squawk, the raven slammed into Madeline Quilleran's perfectly coiffed head with a gooey splat, and she lost her concentration with a yelp. Light flared in dying sparks between her and the bug. I noted the moment when Yen realized he was no longer being held in that room.

"Now!" I screamed to Lea.

She yanked her hands forward and threw a full-blown spell, written in shimmering green strands the width of spider silk, over the bug. Before he could even think about hightailing it through the door, the magic wrapped around him like an angry, wriggling cocoon.

"*Resilio!*" Lea screamed, and the cocoon flared into soft green light, sending the compressed bug to the top of Yen's desk.

Bandy Joe pounced on it, grabbing the webbing and slipping the whole mess into the metal box. He slammed the sliding shutter closed to lock Yen inside.

A moment of quiet relief swelled between us.

Then Lea and I and Joe shared a look and a smile. "We got him," I finally said.

"That was the clumsiest..."

We all turned to look at the woman standing across the room. "...most inept, excuse for magic wrangling I've seen in all my decades as a practicing witch..."

I flushed with embarrassment. "Hey, we got it done."

She shook her head. "Barely. And only because I was here to throw a magical padlock on him."

I opened my mouth to argue...and then noticed Madeline's hair and the words slid right out of my brain.

One whole side of her head was be-slimed, her usually perfect silky dark hair glued to her cheek and neck and sticking up in the back where Rasputin's wing must have disrupted it in trying to extract himself.

About the raven... I looked around, not seeing him. Glancing down to the floor, I was shocked to see Rasputin lying on his back, his feet straight up in the air and his beak open on a silent scream.

Oh, my goddess, she didn't! My accusing glare found the witch's face. "You killed him!"

She rolled her eyes.

Okay, I was starting to get a complex.

"He's fine. He passed out from the shock of

hitting me in the midst of a powerful spell. He'll be fine."

I closed my eyes in relief. If he'd been killed that would have been on me. Rasputin was annoying, but that didn't mean I wanted him dead.

Though seeing him slimed and humiliated had been tons of cheeky fun.

"Nice try on the deflection, witch," Bandy Joe said. "You'll be answering to the Universe about your role in all this. You hopped a dimension, illegally, and came to warn another PTB who was trafficking in illegal artifacts that he was about to get caught."

To my surprise, Madeline didn't deny any of the charges. "I'll answer to the Universal Court. Have no fear, Keeper."

But she was staring at me as she made the promise to Bandy Joe. I couldn't help wondering why. There almost seemed to be a message in her gaze. One that I was definitely not receiving.

Maybe it was being blocked by all the stinky goop.

I didn't even care. I just wanted to stand in the shower for two days and then go home. Wicked and I had to check on Mr. Slimy...

Wicked!

My head shot up. "Where's my cat?"

We all looked around, but he was nowhere to be found.

Not again!

I rushed out of the office, calling his name. Hopefully, he hadn't gotten out of the building when all the customers had run screaming from the place.

"Wicked!"

"Avast ye!" said a familiar, shrill voice. "Pull ye toes from the gangplank."

My gaze shot toward a short hallway leading off the lobby. I ran toward the sound of SB's voice. What in the world was he up to? "SB, do you have Wicked?"

I heard water running as I came through the door. Wicked was lying across a round table in the center of what looked a break room of some kind. He was damp but clean, and his fur was fluffy, like the down of a baby bird.

He was gnawing on a bagel with cream cheese.

"Wicked..."

"Fiddle de de and fiddle de dum, 'tis a pirate's joy to bathe in his rum..."

I narrowed my gaze on the bottle that was tipped on its side at the edge of the sink, making sure it was soap and not rum. The water was running from the faucet in a steady stream, sending the stinky detritus of our battle with Yen down the drain amid copious amounts of bubbles.

There was no way the parrot had thought of bathing in the sink. It had to be Wicked's doing.

I couldn't even scold my cat for eating somebody's leftover breakfast.

He was just too cute for me to be mad.

I unlocked the door to *my* Croakies and stepped inside, taking a beat just to enjoy the familiar scent, a mix of the floral fragrance Sebille carried with her wherever she went, and the welcoming aroma of old and new books.

Wicked bounded past me, heading toward the connecting door and tapping it with a paw. To my astonishment, the locks snicked and the door swung open.

I shook my head. Every day my cat was becoming more and more powerful. My fanciful notion that he was almost more witch than the witches I knew was becoming less a notion and more a real possibility.

And he was still a baby. Barely a year old.

I shook my head and moved into the store, locking it behind me and engaging the wards for the night. I glanced at the teacup-shaped clock and grimaced. Nine o'clock.

It had taken forever to negotiate the trip out of the other dimension.

There had been reports to be completed, a bad guy to be booked and carted off to Area 51, and then a travel window through the Universe to be negotiated.

At least the actual trip had been fairly quick. The PTB had sent orders down to Bandy Joe that he could use his handy, Bandy little notebook to send me back. He'd told me the notebook was how he'd gotten to *his* Croakies and back with the magic box so quickly.

It was like the Book of Pages, but required a special quill pen to jot down what you needed.

Plus, unlike the Book, Joe's notebook was pocket-sized and icy cool. And I wanted one for Christmas.

It had all been exciting, unnerving and discombobulating. I felt as if I'd been awake for forty-eight hours. I probably had been. Who even knew what day it currently was?

I trudged upstairs, my footsteps heavy and slow on the stairs, and stopped short when I saw my partially-open apartment door.

Someone was in my home!

I realized it could have been Wicked performing his new breaking and entering magics. But I didn't think it was. There was a strong Lavender scent in the air.

Unless the Boogey Man had brought me flowers, I had to have an unwanted visitor.

The air whispered behind me and, without any warning, my hand shot into the air.

Blackbeard's sword smacked into my palm and my fingers folded around it.

I smiled at the blade. "Hello, old friend."

The blade danced in my grip, slicing the air efficiently in front of me. SB landed on my shoulder in a flutter of wings and drifting feathers. "Time ta blow the man down, Lass?"

"I'm not sure. But just in case, look alive."

The bird danced to the edge of my shoulder and back again, wings rustling softly against my hair. "But I be long dead these many decades, ye daft scallywag."

"Right, silly me." I sighed, too tired to deal with the parrot.

I eased up to the doorway and peered around it, sword held in two hands before me in case I needed to act quickly. The room was still. Nothing moved inside. It felt normal and quiet...except for a high-pitched whistling sound.

Realization bloomed in my brain, and was verified as I tried to push the door fully open and it banged up against a chair that hadn't been there when I'd left.

I gritted my teeth, growling under my breath. *Sebille!*

I'd forgotten about the Sprite squatting in my home.

Standing in the doorway, I looked into the mess cluttering my once peaceful and sparsely furnished home and felt like crying.

Who needed so much stuff? It wasn't normal. It wasn't healthy. It wasn't...

I sighed. It wasn't going to continue. I had to get the Sprite a home. And fast.

I released the sword, flinging a strand of keeper magic at it as I searched for a pathway to my bathroom.

"A fair eve'n to ye, Lass," SB said as he followed the sword back to its perch on top of the artifact shelves.

"Night, SB," I said, yawning. I found a narrow path through the clutter, only bumping my knees and gouging my shins a few times on the way to the bathroom.

Wicked was already curled up on his pillow, immune to the whistling snores and claustrophobic chaos of our home.

I glared at Sebille as I passed her couch. She was sprawled on her back, one arm flung over her face and her long, fire-red hair splayed around her on the pillow. One skinny leg was draped over the low back of the couch and the other stuck out from the blanket, her foot resting on the floor. She was wearing a striped onesie that reminded me of the striped socks she favored. Tucked neatly beside the couch was a pair of red slippers to complete the strange outfit.

I shook my head, feeling affection rising to replace the anger.

She was a pain in my behind. But she *was* entertaining.

Still, I decided I'd use my outside voice when I

sang the *Make me a Magic Muffin Mister* song to flush my magical toilet.

If it woke her up...so be it. It only seemed fair, since her whistling snores would probably keep me up all night anyway.

The thought had me grinning as I closed the bathroom door behind me.

17

A GRYM STATE OF AFFAIRS

*D*espite my expectation of being kept awake all night, I slept like the newly dead. The sun was beating against my eyelids when I came awake, and something soft, warm, and rumbly was pressed against my side.

I rubbed my eyes open and looked down to find Wicked snuggling against me, purring in his sleep. Grinning, I rolled over and tugged him closer, kissing the top of his fragrant head. His eyes came open and he yawned widely, batting me on the nose without claws for waking him up.

I laughed. "Time to get up, sleepyhead. There are dust bunnies to conquer and artifacts to wrangle."

He stretched, yawning again, and then hopped down from the bed, disappearing into the closet where I kept his litter box to do his morning business.

I rolled out of bed, succumbing to my own yawn, and trudged toward the bathroom. I jolted to a stop at the terrifying vision sitting at my kitchen table.

Sebille's hair was a tangled mess, sticking up on one side in a giant knot and a crusty glue of what was probably drool plastering it to her cheek on the other. She was still wearing the weird onesie and she'd jammed her feet into the bright red slippers. There was a cup of tea in front of her, alongside a copy of the Enchanted Gazette. She was frowning.

"Morning," I said, determined to make the best of her presence until I could get her out of my space.

Inexplicably, her frown deepened.

"What's wrong?"

We hadn't gotten another order for artifact wrangling. I would have known. It would have been hard to miss since tiny gnomes would have been making shish kabob out of my brain with pickle forks if we had.

She shoved the paper toward me. I looked down at the headline blaring across the front page. *Another Murder in Enchanted*, the headline screamed.

"Oh no," I said, feeling sad. "What's going on in our quaint little town?"

Sebille took a sip of her tea, her expression ominous. "Read the article."

I started to argue. I really needed to sing the Magic Muffin song first and I needed a cup of tea in the worst way, but something in Sebille's eyes had me biting back the complaint. My bladder could wait a few minutes.

I quickly scanned the article, a lump of dread moving into my belly as I got to the part I assumed had put the scowl on Sebille's freckled face. "The victim was discovered by a local businessman, Theopolis Gargantu, next to his pawn business, Enchanted Collateral," I read aloud. I glanced at Sebille. She lifted vivid red brows.

"You don't think Theo killed him... Do you?"

Sebille sighed. "Keep reading."

I dropped into a chair and pulled the paper close. "Police aren't releasing the victim's name at this time, but one key piece of information did find its way to our reporter's notice. The victim had a single gold coin clutched in one hand when he was found."

The knot in my belly exploded to consume my entire middle section. I swallowed bile as I realized my work with the gold-creating purse was still far from done. I might have caught the mastermind of the artifact's release into the human population, but I still didn't know who Yen had been working with.

And I had no idea who currently had possession of the artifact.

"That thing's going to keep killing people," Sebille said softly. There was no accusation in her tone. No censure. But I supplied that all on my own. While I'd been gallivanting across the Universe, people had been getting mixed up with the artifact it was my job to collect.

I suddenly felt guilty for having slept so well the night before. "Oh, Sebille. What have I done?"

She shook her head, staring at her tea. "It's not your fault. You've been doing your best to find out what's going on."

The fact that she was defending me told me how dire it was. "Stop being nice to me," I snapped. "You're making me feel like the end of the world is nigh."

She sighed again.

A strident clang sounded from outside my apartment. It was the warning chime in the artifact library that someone was at the book store entrance, trying to get in.

Sebille's lustrous green gaze lifted to mine. "That will be Detective Grym. He's been calling all morning."

I glanced around for my phone, not finding it.

"It's in the bathroom. I finally silenced it about an hour ago."

I shoved to my feet. "I'll get dressed. Can you let him in?"

———

D etective Grym stared down at me through dark eyes filled with anger.

I stared up at him, trying to look like I didn't deserve the anger. I didn't *think* I deserved it, but I wasn't sure, since I had no idea what he was angry about.

Finally, I got tired of his accusing stare. "What can I help you with, Detective?"

His dark brows folded closer together. "I think it's time we worked together instead of at cross purposes, don't you, Naida keeper?"

"Cross purposes? I don't understand."

He finally looked away, jamming his hands on his hips and staring at the floor. "You seem to be at all the murder sites before I am. You've spoken to the victims before I even knew they were victims. I'm starting to wonder if you're not connected in some way that you don't want me to know about."

I couldn't believe my ears. "You're kidding me, right?"

His gaze flashed. Not for the first time, I wondered exactly what the detective was...magically speaking. He definitely gave off an aura of magical involvement, but he'd shown no obvious aptitude beyond the ability to get irritated with me. "I don't kid about murder, Keeper."

"That's your answer right there," I told him.

He blinked and shook his head. "Huh? That I

don't kid about murder? What in tattered lizard thongs does that even mean?"

"I'm a Keeper of the Artifacts, Detective Grym. I'm trying to do my job. Just as, I assume, you're trying to do yours."

"My job would be easier if you didn't keep stepping all over it."

"Maybe if you told me exactly what I've done to mess you up, I can make sure I avoid doing it in the future."

His lips tightened, making the muscles in his neck turn to steel bands. It was a good neck. They were good lips too. In fact, the whole package was good in a well-put-together, pleasing to look at way.

It was just the personality that could use some work.

"You recently visited Enchanted Collateral?"

It was a question, so I answered it. "Yes."

He seemed to be waiting for more. "Um, yes, Detective?"

There was an odd grinding sound that might have involved somebody's teeth. Not mine. My teeth were just fine. I ran my tongue over them to be sure. They were a little fuzzy.

"What were you doing there?" he ground out through the grinding teeth. Waaayyy too much grinding going on. The man needed to drink some Chamomile tea or something.

"Looking for the artifact we discussed at Wo's Chinese Restaurant."

"Why did you think it was at Enchanted Collateral?"

"I didn't."

He lifted a brow in question.

"I wanted to know if it had maybe passed through the pawnshop."

Grym nodded, staring at the floor again. When he glanced up, his face was slightly less taut. "You didn't suspect Theopolis Gargantu of using the artifact?"

It was my turn to frown. "No. Of course not."

"Why?"

"Do you know any giants?"

"I can't say I do, no."

"Well, they're very gentle creatures. Kind and sensitive. I'd be shocked if a giant would ever do something that would cause someone harm."

"So you don't see him killing someone?"

"Absolutely not!"

My response was so emphatic, Detective Grym's eyes widened in surprise. "What about passing the artifact on to a human?"

That was a much grayer area. Theo wouldn't do it if he realized that it would more than likely harm the human. But if the exchange was based, in his mind, strictly on the attainment of goods... "If he didn't understand it might harm them, maybe." I hated even to put that in words, but I was also determined not to lie to the cop. I needed to get that artifact off the streets, and if Grym could help me do it quicker, I'd gladly take his help.

"What did you learn from your trip through the Universe?" Grym asked me.

I blinked in surprise at the abrupt change in conversational direction. I didn't even ask him how he knew where I'd been. I figured he got a daily report on things of magical interest that might affect his job. "What did I learn?" I learned that Madeline Quilleran and her raven were a couple of slug patooties. I learned that supersized stink bugs really ruined my day. And I learned who a second PTB was. But I didn't want to share any of that with Detective Grym, so I relayed the one piece of information I *could* share.

"I found out who released the artifact into the human consciousness."

He cocked his head. "And who was that?"

"Wo Yen's distant cousin, Fu Yen."

His brows lifted in surprise. "A human?"

"No. Fu Yen is a magical creature. He shifted into a giant stink bug while we were there." Okay, so I couldn't resist sharing that.

Grym's lips slowly turned up at the corners. "You're serious?"

"Unfortunately," I grimaced. "Nasty thing. We managed to corral him into an artifact, and the local

KoA turned him over to the PTB Board. Last I heard he was heading to Area 51."

Grym nodded, seeming to get lost in thought. "Okay, that makes sense. It's the connection we needed between the artifact showing up and the first victim."

Since he seemed to have relaxed a bit, I headed across the room and grabbed a couple of cups. "Would you like tea?" I asked the detective.

He nodded. "Please." He leaned a hip against the short counter where our tea stuff was and crossed his arms over his chest. "So I assume it was handed down through the family like an inheritance?"

I nodded, dropping a frog-shaped infuser inside my pretty china pot. I hadn't been able to resist it when I'd spotted it at Lea's shop. And since I'd met Bandy Joe and his frogs, I liked it even more. "I didn't get an order when Yen inherited it because there'd been no problems historically with the artifact up to that point."

"But when he started to get poisoned..."

"I should have been called in to retrieve it." I poured him a cup and handed it to him.

"Should have been?"

"Long story. There was a breakdown in the system, which was why I was sent to the other dimension."

Grym sipped his tea thoughtfully. "His wife took the artifact when he was arrested?"

I blew on my tea. "Yes. I tried to talk her out of using the thing. I knew it was only a matter of time until she was poisoned too."

"Why?"

"Because she is...was...human."

"No, she wasn't. Not completely, anyway. Paula Yen was half Brownie, though I think she'd turned more boggart than brownie by the end. Probably from the effects of the artifact."

I was shocked. "How do you know that?"

He shrugged. "It's my job to know."

When I continued to eye him, he said. "Just trust me on this. She wasn't fully human."

"Okay," I finally said. "Do you think her death was an accident?" I couldn't help remembering the condition of the kitchen. Had the room been destroyed as the result of a struggle? Or had somebody been searching for something? Like, say, a purse that created gold coins?

But Grym's statement that Paula Yen might have turned boggart would also explain the mess. Once a Brownie feels it's been mistreated somehow, they could turn angry and seek retribution. Destruction of the property they'd once taken great care to protect was right in the wheelhouse of possible boggart activities.

He didn't answer immediately. Finally, he settled his teacup onto the counter and scrubbed a hand over his jaw. "I originally thought it might have been suicide."

The shock must have shown on my face because he nodded. "I know, it's a weird way to go. But she knew that kitchen like the back of her hand. She spent hours there alone every night, prepping, cleaning and doing the books for the restaurant. I just couldn't believe she'd accidentally lock herself into the freezer."

"Okay. But suicide…"

"She was clutching a note."

"Oh." That made a huge difference.

"Wrapped around a gold coin."

Oh! "What did the note say?"

"Forgive me."

I frowned. "That's it? Just *forgive me*?"

He nodded.

"Hm."

"Yeah, my sentiments exactly," Grym said. "And then this latest murder happened."

"I just read the story in the paper. You think it's the artifact again?"

"I do. And if that's the case I have to wonder, how did the thing get from Paula Yen's possession to the killer's."

That was a very good question. It pretty much guaranteed she hadn't killed herself.

18

A VERY BAD SCENE

*T*he victim had dropped to his knees and fallen forward, his forehead resting against the brick of the building next to Enchanted Collateral. One hand was splayed against the wall as if he'd tried to keep from hitting it too hard when he fell. The other hung in a fist at his side.

The knuckles of both hands were broken and bloody.

"He put up a fight," I murmured, my eyes stinging with tears for the person who'd been the victim of rampant greed. "The article said he was holding a coin?"

Grym reached over and tugged a rigid finger of the splayed hand, a sheen of gold showed between the fingers.

"Was he holding it? Or did somebody jam it in

there after he died?" I asked, peering closer to try to see if the coin matched the ones I'd seen before.

Grym answered a bit distractedly. "That hasn't been determined yet." Frowning at a dark mark along the opposite brick wall, the detective's gaze slipped upward, following the wide swath of charred surface. "What do you suppose caused this?"

I followed his line of sight, shaking my head. "No clue. But look at his clothes."

Grym walked over and peered down at the man's ragged slacks and shabby jacket. The front of his shirt was also tattered, the edges black with filth. "I'd say he's a homeless guy."

"How did a homeless guy get hold of a gold coin?" I asked the detective.

"That's part of what's perplexing about this scene." He returned to the black mark on the wall, running his fingers over it and then holding the soot-covered fingers to his nose. "This is a char mark. There was a fire here."

"Fire? In just one strip up the wall?"

"A flamethrower, maybe?"

I had a thought, returning to the body, I knelt down and leaned close, sniffing. "I smell smoke here too. Could this..." I indicated the blackened and ragged clothing, "...be from burning instead of natural wear?"

"If that was the case you'd think the skin underneath would be burned too."

I carefully tugged the shirt apart in the center, seeing discolored but healthy skin beneath. "There's soot but no damage."

"That tells me it was magical flame," Grym said, his expression fitting his name. "Dragon."

I stood, rubbing my arms against a sudden chill. I'd never come up against a dragon before, and I'd hoped I never would. They were deadly and rigidly focused on protecting any loot they claimed as their own. "I hope you're wrong."

"So do I," Grym said. He called out to the people waiting at the mouth of the alley and pointed to the body. The morgue crew rolled the black-bag-covered gurney over and carefully removed the body. The coin clattered to the ground as they lifted the body from the wall.

Grym reached down, his hands covered in latex gloves, and picked it up. His expression hardened as he looked at it.

The detective held the coin up for me to see. "Still think I'm wrong?"

The figure of a dragon breathing fire was molded into the face of the coin.

It was a figure I'd seen before. "Slimy frog flip flops," I swore. He'd been right.

"I need to talk to Theo," I told Grym.

"Theo?"

Pointing toward Enchanted Collateral, I started walking toward the mouth of the alley. "The owner of the pawnshop. If there's been a dragon hanging around here, he'll know."

———————

Theo was standing in his office door, talking to the woman who'd been borderline rude to us the last time we'd visited.

He looked up as Detective Grym and I approached and his gaze narrowed. He said something to the woman, handing her the sheet of paper they'd been discussing, and then turned a smile on us. "Naida keeper. Two times in a week. How did I get so lucky?"

The pale gray gaze of the muscular woman scratched over Grym and me, her features tight with distrust.

Grym tugged out the badge he wore on a chain around his neck. "Detective Wise Grym with the Enchanted Police Department. How are you today, sir?"

Theo's eyes filled with pleasure, which I found strange. He hurried forward and wrapped Grym's offered hand in an encompassing grip. "Detective. It's an honor. I'm a regular donor to the police fund. I appreciate all your hard work."

I fought an eye roll at that. Theo was such a suck-up. "We wondered if we could talk to you a moment," I told the Jolly, not-so-green giant.

"Of course. Of course. In my office?"

Grym nodded as I grimaced. The last thing I wanted was for Grym to see Theo cart me through the furniture jungle like a helpless child.

"Um, maybe we could just talk out here."

Grym gave me a strange look. "Actually, I'd prefer to keep this private." He skimmed the hostile-eyed employee a look over my shoulder, and I turned to find her glowering at us.

Theo sighed. "I apologize. Birte's very protective. She had a...bad experience with the police once." He shook his head, motioning toward his office door with a smile. "After you."

I tugged on Grym's sleeve, stopping him. "Have you ever been inside a giant's home artifact before?"

He frowned. "No. Why?"

I felt the heat of Theo at my back, his wall of flesh pressing me forward.

"Just look alive."

Grym held my gaze for a beat longer and then shook his head and stepped through the door.

A table shot past just as he stepped into the room, erasing him from view like a wiper skimming water droplets from a windshield.

All that was left behind was a muffled yelp and a meaty thump.

I gave Theo a glare.

He lifted his hands in a helpless sign. "I can't control them," he said. But there was a spark of something in his eyes that looked way too much like amusement for my comfort.

I stopped in the doorframe and looked both ways before entering.

There was no sign of Grym, but I heard some groaning in the corner and found him half under and half behind a glossy old buffet.

"Are you okay?"

His response was another groan.

I started to crouch down to see him, and one of the buffet drawers shot out, barely missing my head. I straightened, sighing. Sticking out my hand, I said, "Hello. I'm Naida."

The drawer came open again, more gently the second time, and the knob found my palm.

I gave it a squeeze. "If you don't mind, I just need to help my friend out of there."

The doors in the front of the big piece of furniture opened and closed and the buffet skidded sideways, its legs screeching loudly on the hard floor.

"Um, thanks." That wasn't quite what I'd been suggesting but it worked.

Grym was huddled in the space the buffet had deserted, a knot already growing under his dark hair.

I crouched down. "Can you stand up?"

He turned his head, grimacing, and touched the knot on his head. "That depends on what just hit me."

My lips twitched. "I'm not sure, but I think it was a game table."

His mouth fell open. "Did somebody shove it at me?"

"No. It shoved itself."

"That's..."

A floor lamp bent over my shoulder, the pull chain gaily waving. The lamp's lacy shade nodded a greeting to the downed cop.

"...impossible," he finished. "Is that lamp nodding at me?"

"I believe it is." I gave up trying to hold my grin back. "Welcome to Theo's artifact."

He sighed. "I don't suppose there's any way to keep this stuff from running me over again?"

"Nope. Thus my warning to..."

"Look alive." He nodded, taking my hand and allowing me to help him stand. "Got it."

It took a few minutes and required Theo running interference for the last two-thirds of it, but Grym and I finally sat down in front of Theo's big desk.

It turned out the artifacts were just as excited to meet an Enchanted cop as Theo had been.

The good news was that Grym's popularity took the pressure off me. I was able to move to my chair with nary a duster dustup or armchair altercation.

Theo motioned to the tea set and it delivered steaming cups in record time, settling them gently into our hands.

I sipped mine as I swung my dangling legs, then set it down on the wooden seat of the chair beside my hip to cool.

"I'm sure you know about the murder in the alley," Grym said.

I frowned at his abrupt launch into the ugly business at hand.

Theo frowned too. "Yes. Terrible thing. The homeless population seems to be expanding in Enchanted. Poor folks. I wish I could do more to help them."

I appreciated his tender sentiments, but his words surprised me. I personally hadn't met any homeless in Enchanted. The town had a pretty good infrastructure set up to take care of anyone who needed help. "Have you helped them before?" I asked, sipping from my tea and finding it cool enough to drink. And delicious.

He shrugged. "I give them food and clothing. And anything else I can do." His gaze slid toward the door to his office and then jerked back down to his desk. "No one should have to live like that. Without...stuff."

Ah, that was the crux of it. To a giant, not being surrounded by way too much stuff would be the worst kind of hell.

He'd love it at my house these days.

The thought made me grimace. I hadn't had time

to find Sebille an apartment again. Maybe if I went to her previous landlord and threw myself on his mercy he'd relent and let her move back.

Or I could bribe him with my ration of apples and peaches from Lea's greenhouse...

Nah. I'd rather live in clutter, my ears ringing with Sebille's whistling snores, than give up the crisp, sweet fruity goodness.

"Did you know the victim?" Grym asked him.

"No. Should I?"

It was a strange question. Theo's furtive glance toward the door seemed strange too. Putting two and two together, I asked, "That employee out there—Birte?—is she homeless?"

Theo shook his head too fast and too hard. "Not at all. Would you like more tea?"

"Theo?"

He sighed. "Don't say anything to her about it. She's very sensitive."

"Is it possible she knew the victim?" Grym continued, still singing the same song.

Theo frowned at the pen on his desk. It had risen up onto its point and was dancing across the blotter, leaving a truly captivating pattern of swirling dots behind on the pristine paper surface.

Theo grabbed the pen, his jaw tightening, and shoved it into a drawer.

I felt my eyes go wide and was stricken with a

burning desire to rescue the pen from its dark prison. "Theo, we need your help. This artifact is killing people. The sooner we find it, the sooner we can stop the carnage."

He sighed. "Okay, yes. Birte might know him. She's friends with some of the homeless."

"You mentioned your employee had a run-in with the police. Was it for violence?" Detective Grym asked.

Theo's wide face paled. "No. Oh, no, not anything like that. She just...liberated something from the curb she thought was being thrown away."

Grym let one dark eyebrow climb his brow. "She stole something?"

Theo frowned. "It was an honest mistake, I assure you."

Silence fell as Grym jotted a note in his little notebook. When he looked up, it was clear he was ready to sing a different tune. "Mr. Gargantu, have you seen any dragons around here?"

Theo looked appalled. He turned his shocked expression to me. "Absolutely not! Tell him, Naida keeper."

I grimaced. "Giants and dragons can't stand each other."

Theo nodded enthusiastically. "Dragons are foul creatures. They're hoarders of the worst kind."

I watched Grym try to hide a shocked grimace. I

couldn't really blame him. I mean, Theo was the king of hoarders.

Packed pot, meet cluttered kettle.

"We saw definite signs of magical fire on and around the victim," I told the giant.

Theo was shaking his head again. "It's not possible. If one of those tyrants was hanging around my place, I'd know it. And I'd turn its nasty hide into lizard-skin boots."

I didn't doubt he would.

Grym looked at me and said the only three words that were guaranteed to make me hyperventilate. "We're done here."

To his credit, he didn't look any happier about the return trip to the door than I was. We both sat staring at the all-too-distant exit for a moment.

Maybe it wouldn't be so bad to have Grym see the giant carry me out.

Theo stood, grinning. "I'll run interference again."

Grym looked relieved to a comic level. "Good. Thanks."

Fifteen minutes later we emerged. I was sporting a new bruise on my hip from an overzealous bar stool, and Grym was picking copy paper from his teeth...don't ask.

He looked at me as Theo closed himself inside his office, leaving us to question his employees without him. "The next time you know I'm heading into a giant blunder, pun intended, how about you give me a little better warning than 'Look alive', huh?"

I fought my grin. "Got it."

19

YER DRAGON ME DOWN

*Y*oung Penny was on a break at the moment, so we headed toward the ever-friendly Birte. She was crouched behind a low glass cabinet, moving old German beer steins around inside the dusty glass. She looked up as we approached, her heavy brows lowering and her bottom lip sticking out with displeasure. "What?"

I happily left Grym to deal with the cranky woman.

He showed her his badge. "I was wondering if you could answer some questions for us."

She stood, an enormous stein still clutched in her beefy fist as if she wouldn't mind pummeling us with it. "Am I under arrest?"

Grym blinked in surprise. "Did you do something illegal?"

Her brows lowered further. "From my experience, that isn't always a requirement for getting arrested."

Grym looked at me and I bit back a sigh. "Look, Birte, I'm sure you heard about the murder in the alley…"

"I didn't kill him."

I nodded. "We just wanted to ask…"

"I don't know anything about it."

Biting back irritation, I tried again. "We just thought you might…"

"I don't know him."

"Gargoyle nail clippers, woman!"

Grym's eyes went wide at my explosion.

I ignored him. "Stop cutting me off! We just wanted to ask you…"

"If I killed him?"

My mouth slammed shut.

"If I knew him?"

I looked at Grym. He had a peculiar pinched aspect to his face.

"If I know anything about the murder?"

I sighed. "Okay, that covers it, but…"

"Look, yes, I'm homeless. That's not a crime, is it?"

Grym opened his mouth to respond, and she held up her hand. "Don't bother answering that. It's not a crime as far as I know. I don't hurt anybody. I don't break any laws. I just live my life. I don't have any friends. I don't have any enemies. I'm just surviving." Her eyes were suspiciously bright by the end of her verbal explosion. "Now, please. Just leave me alone."

Grym and I shared a look. He nodded. "Thank you for..."

"Go."

He went. But I found my feet couldn't move, despite my brain telling me they should. "You're wrong," I finally told her. She looked surprised, but for once, she didn't try to respond before I did. "You have a really good friend in Theo. And if you're doing something wrong, you're hurting him. And that's just unacceptable."

I left her struck mute by my words. But I didn't care. I didn't like the whole, "poor me" routine. We all had our problems. But we all had the same opportunities to make the best of our lives. From where I stood, Birte was taking the easy route. She was hiding behind the giant chip on her shoulder as an excuse to not embrace the benefits she did have.

And that was just sad.

I exited the store to find Grym staring at the roofline.

"What?" I asked, turning around and staring up at it with him.

"I want to go up there."

I chuckled, "You want to embrace your inner gargoyle?"

He winced instead of laughing as I'd expected.

Apparently, the interaction with Birte had soured his mood.

I totally understood. It had definitely soured mine.

My gaze skimmed away from him, focusing on the woman coming up the street behind Grym. "Penny."

Grym turned and watched the pretty young college student stride quickly toward us, her sleek black hair shining in the afternoon sun. She was smiling and taking dancy little steps. I realized she was listening to music on the earbuds I could barely see in her ears.

I took off in her direction, intending to intercept her before she got too close to Enchanted Collateral. Grym's heavy footsteps sounded behind me.

Penny jerked to a stop when she spotted us, laughing as she threw us a cheerful wave and then tried to step around us. Her laugh slipped away as we blocked her. I noted the moment she realized we were there to talk to her. Penny's green eyes widened slightly. A cautious smile lifted the corners of her mouth as she tugged the earbuds from her ears. "Hi."

I returned the smile, taking the lead as Grym stood silently at my back. A daunting presence I hoped didn't scare my quarry away. "Hey, Penny. How are you?"

Wariness filled her gaze at my use of her name.

Suspicion cleared as she recognized me. "You're a friend of Theo's. I've seen you in the shop."

"I am." Offering her my hand, I introduced myself. "Naida Griffith. This is Grym."

He waved and smiled, staying silent. Smart man. He'd figured out I wanted to handle the younger woman carefully.

"We just spoke to Theo and Birte and we wanted to get your thoughts."

Her expression compressed into sadness. "The man in the alley." She nodded, sighing. "Poor devil. Do you know what happened to him?"

"Not yet," Grym said. "We were hoping maybe you could tell us something that would help."

She stared at him a long moment and then crossed her arms over her chest, her attitude filled with anger. "Birte had nothing to do with that man's death."

I fought to keep my expression neutral. "Nobody's accusing her…"

"She might be a bit brusque, unfriendly, and sometimes downright rude…"

Way to jump to the other woman's defense, I thought grimly.

"…but she's really a pussycat down deep."

"How deep?" Grym asked.

Penny blinked. "What do you mean?"

"I mean, are her layers deep and complex enough to offer just the slightest possibility that she might harm someone she felt was a danger to her?"

"Or maybe someone she cared about?" I added.

"What's this about, really?" Penny asked, her hostility easing a bit. "You don't really think Birte killed that man, do you?" She skimmed a gaze from me to Grym and then laughed gaily. "Or you think Theo killed him? That man wouldn't hurt a fly. And if you think it was me..." She lifted her arms with a sparkle in her eye. "Look at me. My friends call me stick arms." She pointed to her skinny legs, more like Sebille's bony limbs than my own, too-meaty ones. "The joke at school is that I have corners instead of knees." She shook her head. "I don't even know the guy who was killed, but unless he's a tiny thing I doubt I would have been able to kill so much as a spark of interest in him. You're barking up the wrong tree."

Grym had been studying her intently as she spoke, his expression blank.

When she stopped talking, he took a step closer and lowered his voice. "You have magic."

She paled, blinking rapidly. "I...um..."

I narrowed my gaze on her, seeing nothing. Why was it that everybody but me could seemingly see magic in people when they were trying to hide it?

"Penny?" Grym prompted.

She wrung her fingers together and sighed. "Don't tell Theo."

I thought the request was a strange one. If she had magic she surely knew he was a giant. A non-magic person could navigate his office without difficulty. The artifacts would never show themselves to an unaware human. But if she had magic, she'd have to enter his office wearing bubble wrap and roller skates or risk bruises and copier sheet mayhem as Grym and I had.

"I'm half-Elf. My mother was Elvin. But I don't want Theo to know. He doesn't really trust Elves." She shrugged and bit her lower lip. "Please?"

"There's nothing you can tell us about the victim or his murder?" Grym asked again.

"Nothing. I know Birte knew him. She was upset when she heard he was dead. But I don't hang with the home-free crowd so I wouldn't know him."

"Home free?" I asked.

She nodded. "Theo thinks they're homeless, but they all have homes. Or had them once. They choose to live free on the streets, without the weight of paying bills and all that. Like Birte."

"Birte has a home?"

"Somewhere, yes. She's never told me where it is, but I've overheard her and Theo talking. She's not nearly as pathetic as she seems," Penny said with the coldness of youth.

"Thanks for your help," Grym told her. "We might need to ask you more questions in the coming days."

She shrugged. "You know where to find me." She stepped around us and headed for Enchanted Collateral.

"What do you think?" I asked Grym.

His gaze had found the roofline once again. "I think Miss Birte lied to us about knowing the victim. I also think she has a lot of secrets for someone who supposedly is just trying to mind her own business and survive."

I nodded. I'd thought the same thing. I noted Grym's lack of interest in my response. "You're still thinking you want to go up there?"

"I am." He scanned me a quick look. "Wait here," he barked as he headed back into the alley.

"Not a chance," I told him. I was curious about what he had in mind.

He headed for the metal fire escape hanging off the side of Enchanted Collateral's alley wall. It stopped about ten feet from the ground. "We'll need a ladder."

Ignoring me, Grym jumped into the air, his hands wrapping around the base of the structure and dragging it down with his weight.

"Or not," I said, giving his average height, strongly made physique another look. "Any chance you're a grasshopper shifter?"

He chuckled and I was happy for the sound. He seemed to be regaining his good mood.

"Not even close."

My phone rang as Grym started climbing the fire escape. I stopped on the second step, looking at the screen. It was Sebille.

She never called me. Something must be wrong... "Hello, Sebille? What's wrong? Is Wicked okay? Rustin?"

"Geesh! Unscrew a nerve," she said with clear disgust. "Nothing's wrong. I just wondered when you'd be home."

I blinked in surprise. "Why? Do you need to go somewhere? You can just lock up. I should be home soon."

"I'm not going anywhere. I just..."

Her hesitation made my pulse spike again. "Something is wrong, isn't it? I'll come right home..."

"Naida! I just wanted to know because...well...I cooked dinner."

Well, I'll be a giant's toothbrush. Sebille was calling to find out when I'd be home for dinner? My world was truly warped beyond repair. Maybe I'd accidentally returned to the wrong dimension. "Who are you, and why are you wearing my assistant's striped socks?" That last part was a guess, but I figured it was a pretty safe one.

She sighed. "It's no big deal, Naida. I was making some for me and I just thought I'd make enough for both of us."

I wanted to scream. She was getting way too

comfy in my house. That just couldn't happen. "I...
I'll be home soon. I've got to go."

I quickly disconnected. The first thing I'd do...as
soon as I ate the dinner Sebille had cooked for me...
was get on my computer and find her a place to live.

I didn't care if it took all night. I was going to get
Sebille out of my apartment. Before she decided she
liked it there most of all.

Unless I could talk her into becoming home
free. Hm...

I ran up the fire escape stairs, determined to
make short work of whatever Grym was up to, and
jolted to a halt at the top.

Grym had taken only one step off the stairs. He
was rigid, his hands closed into fists and his shoulders like rock.

"What is it?" I asked, easing around him so I
could see what he was seeing.

I stared at it for a long moment, not entirely sure
what I was seeing.

Then it clicked.

It was a nest.

A really big nest. Bulging with lots of junk and
stuff.

It was a dragon's nest.

"Holy lizard scales."

Grym scrubbed a hand over his jaw. "Does
anybody on this roof really believe the giant didn't
know this was here?"

I grimaced. He made a very good point. "Theo lied to us."

Grym nodded. "There seems to be a lot of that going on." He walked over to the enormous nest and stood at the edge, peering over a two-foot-high rim of branches and cloth to the pile of random objects in the center. "We're going to need to search this for the artifact."

I stood beside him, my stomach clenching at the thought. The stench coming up from the mass of stuff was epic. It made the stink bug goo at the other Croakies pale by comparison.

My hand found my nose, and I made a soft noise of disgust. "Does a dragon poo in its nest?"

Grym scanned me a look. "I have no idea. But it's doubtful. I think that's a combination of rotting food, old gym socks..." he pointed toward a hardened gray sports sock in the center, "and the dragon's natural smell."

My nose wrinkled of its own accord. I didn't blame it. "If that's their natural smell I'm surprised they ever find a mate. I know skunks who smell better." A natural comparison because the smell was a bit skunky, with overtones of dead fish, burnt amber and...oddly enough...a tinge of Basil.

Grym sucked in a breath and climbed over the lip of the nest.

I put a hand on his arm, stopping him.

The detective grinned. "If you're going to tell me

to look alive again I might pinch your arm really hard."

I snorted out a laugh. "Well, yeah. But in more visceral terms...what happens if the dragon comes back while we're digging around in its stuff?" It was a fair question. I didn't know much about dragons, but I knew they were very territorial creatures.

"It won't," Detective Grym said as he stepped down inside the nest. A squishing sound caused him to jerk his foot up and he grimaced down at the thick, white paste coating the sole of his shoe.

It smelled minty fresh.

"Toothpaste," I told him, trying not to smile.

He lifted the foot and tried to scrape it off on the rough nest wall. "The dragon won't be returning before dark."

"How do you know that?" I asked, frowning.

"A dragon leaves its nest by day to avoid discovery. But it always returns shortly after nightfall, usually with more..." His lip curled. "...stuff."

He took two steps into the nest and turned back to me. "Coming?"

Argh!!! "Yes." But as I stepped my first foot into the nest, I couldn't help thinking that Sebille was going to be mighty peeved when I didn't make it home in time for dinner.

My second thought was that the first thought felt really strange in a distinctly uncomfortable way.

And my third thought was to wonder what I had

just stepped down on that felt thick and fleshy and not a little bit slimy.

An hour later, filthy and exhausted, I climbed from the nest and stepped down onto the flat roof.

Waves of stench wafted from the dragon's lair as the final rays of heat from the too-warm day broiled it from the top and baked it in the heated asphalt from the bottom.

Half of the nest's contents were strewn about the roof. The other half was too slimy or too tender to lift out. We'd left that on the bottom, but not without getting a good coating of the rotting stuff as we searched through the mire.

We'd found everything from nose hair clippers to a purple bow-tie with bright yellow polka dots in the nest.

But no gold-coin-making artifact.

I moved to the edge of the roof to get away from the smell, and then realized the smell went with me.

I was wearing it.

Stink bug boogers!

Grym climbed out a moment later, looking up at the lowering sun. "He'll be back soon. You should go."

I frowned. "What about you?"

He shook his head. "I'll be fine. I need to confront the dragon and find out where he put the artifact."

"I can't leave you here by yourself."

Grym smiled, his handsome face streaked with dirt and glossy with slime. "I'm a police officer, Naida. I can take care of myself."

"Against a dragon?" I really didn't like the shrieking quality of my voice, but I couldn't believe he thought he could battle a dragon on his own. "It will kill you, Grym."

He shook his head. "I'll be fine. I have..." He shook his head. "I'll be fine. Go home, Naida keeper. Get a shower." He wrinkled his nose, grimacing, and I smacked him on the arm. An array of shiny droplets shot away from the strike zone and landed on the roof with a soft splat.

"Are you sure?"

He nodded, indicating the ladder. "I'm going to pull that up when you're down. I don't want anybody to climb it and accidentally find themselves in the middle of trouble up here."

I nodded and, after one last, questioning look, descended the ladder and headed out of the alley.

That was when I realized I'd ridden there with the Detective.

I didn't have my car.

I called the shop and Sebille answered. "Yeah?"

Okay, she was peeved. "Hey. It's me. Sorry about dinner."

Silence met my apology. I started to rub my face and then got a look...and a sniff...of my hand and changed my mind. "Grym had me digging through a dragon's nest looking for the artifact."

I could almost hear her jaw softening a bit on that news. "A dragon's nest? In Enchanted?"

"Yeah, isn't that just the frog's flip flops?"

She snorted. "Why are you calling?"

Oh, yeah. "I need a ride back. Grym's staying to talk to the dragon."

There were a few beats of stunned silence. "You're going to leave him there by himself?"

"Of course not. But I need to grab a shower and a few other things. Would you send Berbie to pick me up? Please?"

"On one condition."

Oh, oh. "What's the condition?"

"I want to come too. I've always wanted to see a dragon."

"Do you have fire-proof wings?"

She snorted again. "Of course. Have you met my brothers?"

20

AND INTO THE FIRE

*B*erbie had even more pep in his pistons than usual. He must have been feeding off the nervous energy thrumming through his leather interior. We'd made it across town in a record five minutes, never taking a turn on more than two wheels. I was pretty sure the little car was somehow manipulating the traffic lights of Enchanted because we seemed to make every light with very little green to spare.

But as he screeched to a stop on the street in front of Enchanted Collateral, I realized whatever time we'd saved, it hadn't been enough.

Fire arced into the sky above the roof. Cinders floated in the air around the building, and smoke was thick enough to make it hard to breathe.

I was a little surprised the Enchanted Fire Department hadn't been called.

"I'll go up and get the lay of the land," Sebille said. A burst of energy transformed her into her Sprite form and she shot upward, toward the action high above.

As I jumped out of Berbie, throwing a request for him to wait at the curb over my shoulder, the front door of EC opened and Theo came out, his wide, usually ruddy face the color of the ash accumulating on the sidewalk. "Naida keeper! Thank the goddess you're here. You have to help her."

I should have been surprised by his words, but I wasn't. "You knew all along, didn't you?"

Theo wrung his hands. "She didn't kill anybody. She couldn't have."

After seeing the cold glares Birte sent Grym and me every time we visited the pawnshop, I wasn't so sure about that. "You should have told us she was nesting on the roof." I frowned, realizing if he had, his employee might not be fighting for her life above our heads. "Besides, I'm more worried about Detective Grym. If she hurts him..." *Or worse*, I couldn't help thinking, "...she'll be in even more trouble than she's in now. You need to convince her to give it up, Theo."

He shook his head, sausage fingers wringing together in front of him. "I can't. The loot is all she has. She's just trying to survive."

"She has a job, doesn't she?" I angrily asked as something clanged hard against the power box high above our heads. A thick burst of flames seared the edge of the roof, sending a fresh spate of flaming wood and the sour stench of heated tar down on us.

Theo's lips compressed into a hard, thin line. "You don't understand..."

"Help me understand," I said. "In shorthand, because I need to get up there and help Grym."

I looked up at a loud buzzing sound. The Sprite was diving down from the roof, tension in every line of her tiny body. "She's got him pinned," Sebille told me, before buzzing back up toward the roof. A beat later, a flash of green light told me Sebille was doing what she could to help.

The roar of an enormous, angry lizard shattered the night and something gray and blocky slammed backward off the roof, barely stopping its downward spiral by digging dense claws into the brick as it fell.

A Gargoyle?

The 'goyle looked down at Theo and me before digging into the brick and scrambling back up to the roof. For just a beat, its yellow gaze had reflected rage at seeing us. I wondered if that rage was directed at me...or at the giant wringing his hands and doing nothing to help.

"Theo!" I yelled as another flash of green light, another roar, and the splintering sound of something structural giving way strummed my very last nerve.

He just stood there, tears sliding down his ashy face.

I threw him a glare and took off running toward the alley. I barely breached the mouth of the narrow space before I remembered the fire escape had been pulled up.

I didn't think I could jump high enough to grab it and pull myself up. I briefly considered calling to Sebille for help. But I hated to disturb her. From the thick columns of fire spearing the night sky and the sound of things being ripped apart, it appeared she and the Gargoyle had their hands full.

Then I realized I didn't need the fire escape. I had Berbie!

Running back toward the street, I yanked the driver's side door open and leaped in behind the wheel. "I need you to use that magical mojo to get us up the side of that building, buddy."

With a happy toot of his horn and several roaring revs of his engine, Berbie took off faster than I'd expected, flinging me back against the seat. I gave a little scream as we hit the curb and went airborne, the front tires striking the side of the brick and slowing with a jolt.

But Berbie revved again, and the tires took hold. I was suddenly clinging in terror to the steering wheel as we went completely vertical.

Two-thirds of the way up, Berbie's efforts seemed to lose steam. I felt gravity sucking on his rear bumper and closed my eyes, envisioning a fiery crash on the sidewalk below. Fortunately, Berbie always did have more will than sense. His engine roared, the rear tires skimming sideways on the warm brick. For just a beat, I was certain we were going to lose our grip and plunge to our deaths.

But one tire caught hold of the uneven surface. And another. And then we were suddenly shooting upward again.

We flew over the top of the building, and, for one terrifying moment I thought we might sail right over it.

Then I had a brand-new terror to confront. The enormous, fire-eyed lizard standing in the center of the wide, flat roof spun around with more speed and agility than it should have been able to conjure, and opened its maw, intending to send us sailing out into thin air on a fat ribbon of fire.

It didn't exactly happen that way. The rock-like gargoyle flew through the air and slammed his heavy body into the dragon, making her stagger backward just enough that her fiery breath missed us.

But, just as I breathed a sigh of relief, I saw the enormous, meaty tail of the thing lifting to smash into us.

"Berbie!" I yelled. "Watch out!" Even as I screamed the warning, I snagged the door handle and shoved the door open, flinging myself out of the little car and hitting the super-heated surface of the roof.

Berbie managed to zig enough to avoid a direct hit, and then zagged toward the edge of the roof and fell over, his horn joyfully beeping as he made a no-doubt too fast but controlled descent.

I had no time to celebrate the little artifact's safety. The roof vibrated under the thunderous impact of the lizard's massive feet. She stomped over to me and looked down, her undersized wings throbbing slowly behind her.

Time slowed as I rolled and jumped to my feet. In my peripheral vision, I saw hundreds of burning piles through a haze of putrid black smoke and realized the dragon's nest had been obliterated.

Pity tightened my chest as Theo's emotion-clogged words played through my mind. *It's all she has...*

Part of me understood the desperation of trying to survive. I'd experienced that desperation first hand, and seen it in the faces of my friends when they'd lost everything. But those feelings didn't excuse murder. They didn't make endangering and then killing humans acceptable.

The dragon was a thing of great beauty. She was more delicate than I'd thought she would be. The scales covering her slender form were a dove gray that flashed iridescent in the light of the fires surrounding her. Her eyes were almond-shaped, large and sloped exotically in a delicate snout topped with small ears that twitched to keep track of everything around it.

A deadly looking double line of spikes ran from between those ears to the tip of her constantly moving tail, growing larger as they flowed down her back and then narrowing again as they reached the tip of her tail. The very end of the tail had an additional spike which was longer than the others and looked as if it could be used to impale its enemies.

Still, I saw no blood on the dragon. Nothing seemed to be burning except the roof and the non-living items on its surface.

And the dragon wasn't trying to kill me. Instead, she cocked her head as she stared down at me, her beautiful eyes a liquid pool of confusion and hurt.

I bit back the urge to apologize.

"Naida keeper," the Gargoyle growled in a deep, gravelly voice. "I told you to go home."

I blinked, my gaze never leaving the dragon, and tried to figure out when I'd spoken to a Gargoyle.

He stomped over to me, his footsteps barely lighter than the much bigger dragon's. "What are you doing back here?"

I risked him a quick glance, staring into the familiar gaze in an unfamiliar, granite-like face. His brow was bigger, the edges more angular, and his cheekbones looked sharp enough to cut flesh. The wide head was sans hair and the body brought to mind the human depiction of a superhero named the Hulk.

But the eyes were still his and the lips, though charcoal gray and chiseled from the stone of his wide, craggy face, were still well-shaped and enticing. "Detective Grym?"

He shrugged. "Nobody is to know," he growled out.

I nodded, having no desire to tell the world the detective was a mythical guardian whose form graced rooflines around the Universe as protection against evil.

Though it made a certain kind of sense. Him being a cop and all.

"She's coming back," a melodious female voice said. I jerked my head toward the dragon and found her still staring at me.

I would have loved to know what she was thinking.

But there wasn't time. "Who's coming?" I asked the dragon.

Her head shot up, her gaze narrowing on the charcoal gray sky in the distance. I listened carefully and heard the distant throb of wings on the sky. "My sister."

I sent Grym a look.

"I'll explain later. The short version is that she and I have come to an agreement. She's going to help us take down her sister."

"Her sister is the killer?" I asked. "The one who gave the artifact to the Yens?"

He nodded. "She was working with Fu Yen..."

I blinked in surprise. "But how?"

"I'll explain later," he shouted as a massive black dragon dove straight toward us from the sky, her silvery jaws opening as she cut through the air like an arrow.

Behind the bright white rows of teeth, fire burned and swirled like in a wood-burning stove, molten against the back of her tongue.

"Get back!" Grym yelled as the molten death flowed over her tongue toward open air. As soon as it mixed with the gases in the atmosphere...

We had just enough time to leap to the side and roll behind the dented and tattered heating unit before the fire hit the sky and shot in our direction.

At the last moment, the smaller dragon shot off the roof and slammed into the bigger one, blocking most of the flame and diverting it harmlessly away from us.

The silver dragon's smaller form was driven backward and down. Both dragons smashed into the roof, skidding across the fiery surface and stopping at the very edge.

The silver dragon was undersized and handicapped by being in a defensive position, but she was determined. And she had some help. Sebille was firing Sprite magic into her opponent to distract and weaken her, while Grym pummeled the dragon's head with his coiled-granite fists.

I suddenly realized I was useless up there. I'd come to help, but I had nothing to help with. My magic wasn't strong enough to do anything to stop the raging black dragon. I looked around for something I could use as a weapon, but everything was destroyed.

I sent out my keeper magics, searching the immediate area for a useful artifact, and nothing happened. A moment passed. And then another. And still, nothing happened.

More wings fluttered on the air above my head. I looked up into the arrogant silver gaze of the raven as he landed on the broken heating element. "Rasputin. What are you doing here?"

His beak opened in a bird-like sneer. "You didn't really believe you had this under control, did you?"

Of course, I hadn't believed that. But I couldn't let him know it. "We're just about done subduing the culprit. You're late to the party. As usual."

The raven made a smug sound, its head cocking as the black dragon threw Grym across the roof to slam against the vestibule door with a snap of her long neck. "Yes. I can tell. Fortunately for your friends, however, you're really doing your part to help."

I wondered if I would be fast enough to grab the

snotty little varmint before he took off into the night sky.

The door opened and I blinked, thinking Grym had somehow knocked it loose.

But a beat later something flew through the door and headed right for me. My mind had barely registered the ornate form of the beer stein I'd seen Birte dusting in the shop earlier as it smacked into my hands.

I glared down at the artifact. "Really? What am I supposed to do with this? Challenge the dragon to a drinking contest?"

Telling myself that the magical universe generally knew things I didn't, I assumed the beer stein had come to me for a good reason.

Shrugging my shoulders, I ran over and hit the black dragon over the head with the stein. It broke into pieces in my hand, slicing the skin of my palm as the dragon reared up with a roar.

I jumped back, cradling my bleeding hand to my belly as the silver dragon pounded her wings and scrambled up from the debris-strewn asphalt.

The black lunged at her, massive white teeth snapping toward her wing, and sent her tumbling across the surface of the roof on a pain-filled cry.

Then the black dragon turned to me.

Something shiny rolled across the roof and pinged against my shoe. I looked down as the shiny gold coin spun like a top and then toppled to the ground, the familiar image of the fire-breathing dragon glowing through the night.

I reached down and picked it up. That was when I realized the roof had gone very still. My gaze slid to the enraged black dragon, finding its fiery gaze focused on the shiny coin between my fingers as if transfixed by the sight.

I remembered reading about dragons in my classes at college, in my *Mythical Creatures in Popular Fiction* class. The class covered the truths and differences in human mythology and I'd learned a lot there.

Mostly that humans had no clue about us.

I remembered the dragon section was really short, mostly consisting of their aggressive instincts when in protective mode. But also that they loved shiny objects above all things.

I processed this information as Grym crawled slowly to his feet. Behind him, I watched Sebille tend to the silver dragon with healing magics, and then, to my utter shock, watched the dragon revert to her human form in a flare of silver energy.

The woman lying on top of the scorched remains of a blanket looked much smaller without her oversized clothing and much paler under the light of a heavy moon.

Birte's gaze was locked on the coin too. "The artifact?" she asked me, tugging the blanket around her naked form and moving forward as if compelled.

"Stay back!" Grym shouted, moving to get between her and the unpredictable black dragon.

Birte didn't seem to hear him. She appeared mesmerized, her gaze locked on a spot on the ground near the black dragon's razor-spiked tail.

I saw the small, leather pouch lying a few inches from the deadly tail and wondered if I could get there before the black dragon realized what I was going for.

I was afraid if I moved, the dragon's attention would be drawn away from the coin and it would attack.

On the other side of the roof, Grym couldn't see the artifact. "What is it, Naida?"

I shook my head, afraid to speak or move.

But Birte was getting dangerously close to that tail. And the Black twitched suddenly, as if becoming aware of her approach.

I was running out of time. I had to do something. I looked at the coin in my fingers. And then at the pouch, probably ten feet away. And did the only thing I could think of to do.

"Come and get it, ugly!" I threw the coin into the air, near the vestibule, and flung myself toward the pouch as the dragon lunged for the gold.

I leaped over the swinging tail, the deadly spike at the end, barely grazing my thigh as I shoved off the roof and arched my body in a dive that I prayed would help me clear the tail. I landed a foot away from the pouch and rolled, grabbing the edge of the roof as I nearly toppled over and plunged to my death.

Unfortunately, momentum had me in its grip. I kept going, my body sailing out into thin air as I screamed for Berbie.

I heard his horn and the revving of his powerful engine, but knew he wouldn't be in time. I sailed out into open sky and closed my eyes, praying the end would be fast.

Then a rocky vise clamped around my ankle and I slammed to a stop, crashing into the side of the building with a pain-filled yelp.

All the blood rushed to my head as I tried to twist around and look up.

Grym's blocky gray face looked over the edge of the roof. "You okay?"

I glowered at him, adrenaline a river surging through my veins. "I'd be better if I wasn't hanging upside down three stories above the street."

Grym blinked. "Oh. Yeah. Sorry." He dragged me back up and over the edge. I rolled to my back, panting from the near miss. "Thanks."

Then I remembered. "The artifact!"

Grym and I turned to find Birte standing with the pouch in one hand, her eyes glazed as she stared at the freshly minted coin in the other.

"Grym..."

He moved, "On it."

But as he started toward her, Birte's human shape wavered, her head snapped up and the ethereal shape of a silver dragon morphed over her small form. Her eyes caught fire and she opened her mouth, roaring as if she'd already transformed.

Grym stopped, growling deep in his throat. "Déjà vu all over again," he muttered.

"No," I said, as the black dragon turned back, the coin I'd thrown nowhere to be seen, and set its gaze on the gold glistening in Birte's now-clawed hand. "This is not going to happen."

I glanced up at the raven, who'd been a silent observer for the last several minutes. "Ras, if you have a purpose for being here, now would be a really good time to set that into motion."

He cawed and it sounded too much like laughter for my comfort. But he flapped his wings and lifted off the top of the vestibule where he'd been waiting for goddess-knew-what.

The raven headed for Birte, flying right at her face, and snatched the coin from her hand.

She roared, a thick ribbon of dark gray smoke coming from her elongated face, and the silver dragon shape thickened around her, a single thought away from blooming completely over her.

A tiny dragonfly flashed past the transforming dragon and a soft green light filtered over her.

Birte's displeasure was cut off mid-roar. Her eyes

rolled back in her head, her dragon form falling away as she toppled to the ground.

"Sweet dreams," Sebille said as she flashed into full size.

I would have enjoyed taking the time to celebrate the end of one problem, at least. Unfortunately, the next problem was already heading for Sebille as she plucked the artifact out of Birte's hand and threw it to me.

I caught it mid-air and held it aloft for the dragon to see. "Over here, ugly."

The dragon's wings lifted, throbbing slowly against the smoke-drenched air. "I'll take any suggestions you have," I screamed to my friends, over the rumble of fire building in the dragon's wide chest.

Honk, honk! Berbie shot over the edge of the roof and became airborne, heading right for the black dragon.

I watched in horror as the dragon's eyes opened wide and its fiery maw opened. "Berbie, no!"

The vestibule door flew open, slamming against the wall behind it. Madeline Quilleran stepped from its belly, her hands lifted and a golden glimmer in her witchy gaze. "*Reducere!*" she yelled, cupping her hands and twisting them inward.

The dragon twitched once, glanced down and lifted its claws as if trying to fend something off, and then compacted in a blip and dropped with a tinny, silly-sounding roar.

Just as she hit the ground, the dragon form fell away, leaving the startling form of Penny behind on the debris-strewn rooftop.

Berbie's tail lights flashed a happy message to me as he dropped over the other side and made another out-of-control but jubilant descent down the building, his horn tooting happily all the way down.

The building was apparently like a roller coaster ride for magical cars.

I grinned at the thought.

Madeline reached back inside the vestibule and came out with a metal box, tugging a window open as Rasputin flew down and carefully plucked the angrily wriggling woman off the roof with his claws. The raven carried Penny over and dropped her through the window, and Madeline slammed it closed. "*Factum est!*"

It is finished.

She glanced toward me and then scanned a look over Sebille before focusing on Grym, lifting an eyebrow with interest. "I see."

She seemed to shake her fascination for Grym off and looked back to me. "I apologize for being late. I had to retrieve this box from Croakies."

Sebille and I shared a look.

"You what?" I asked, astounded on more than one level.

She shrugged. "You didn't know it was there? I saw evidence of your friend Lea's magic around the box. I just assumed…"

I shook my head. "Why would Lea…?"

The witch shook her head. "No time to chat. I need to get this into custody."

"No," I told her. "You need to tell me why you rode my coattails into the Universe and why you were at Fu Yen's office when we got there."

"Don't be tedious, Keeper," Madeline said, looking bored.

"I'd like to know that too," Grym said, coming from the shadows at the side of the roof. He was wearing the slacks he'd had on when I'd left him, and his shirt, which was still unbuttoned. His feet were bare, and I realized he'd slipped away and dressed while I was distracted. He showed Madeline his badge.

She shook her head. "I should have guessed, of course. You have that annoyingly single-minded tendency to want to protect everybody."

He glared at her. "This stays between us, Quilleran."

She flipped her fingers dismissively.

"You haven't answered my question, Madeline," I reminded her.

She gave a long-suffering sigh. "It's PTB business, Keeper." She said my title as if I were little more than dog poo on her shoe. "Well above your magic rating."

"The Universe made it *my* business when they sent me into the other dimension."

"You have a point," she said, surprising me. She looked thoughtful for a moment and then finally nodded. "I don't know much yet, but there's a rot in the center of everything. I've decided someone needs to get to the center of it."

"And you think that someone should be you?" Grym asked, looking unhappy.

She shrugged. "Do you have someone else in mind? Believe me, Detective Grym, if there were some other way, I'd take it. I have a busy life, and I'd prefer to get back to it. But this corruption just keeps getting worse and, if someone doesn't act we're going to have another Dark Rages."

Grym's gaze narrowed. "You believe there are more corrupt PTB?"

"It might even go deeper than that," she told him, watching him carefully as her words sank in.

I have to assume Grym didn't disappoint. His eyes went wide, and his mouth opened in shock. "You think the Universe is corrupt?"

She frowned. "Let's keep that down, Detective. You never know who might be listening."

Fear blossomed like poison in my chest, making my heart physically hurt. "But we got Fu Yen. He was the rot. Wasn't he?"

Madeline shrugged. "Maybe. We'll have to watch and see."

I grabbed onto that with both hands. She was probably wrong. Or maybe she was just fear-mongering. Yen was at the core of the corruption. Bandy Joe's enormous frog didn't lie. The other Lea's scrying magic had pointed to Yen. And he was currently stinking up a cell at Area 51. It had to be him.

"Well, I'm off," Madeline said.

"I'll take the box," Grym said.

She didn't look pleased, but she did hand him the box. "Does that one need to go into the box too?"

I spun to find Birte sitting on the ground. She leaned against the remains of her nest, the blanket tightly wrapped around her. Tears slipped silently down her cheeks. "I don't think so. I'll deal with her."

Madeline nodded once and then turned to Rasputin. "Come, Ras. I'll buy you an ice cream."

The raven took to the air and found her shoulder, his feathers rippling with excitement. "Strawberry?"

Madeline's laughter was girlish and light. I'd never have expected it to come from her. Sebille and I shared another look, grinning.

Grym lifted the box. "I need to get this in the works. I'll bring it back by Croakies in the morning if that's okay."

I nodded. "Thanks for helping me get this," I told

him, lifting the artifact which, judging by the feel of it, had birthed another gold coin.

"What are you going to do with it?"

"It will be locked up in the toxic magic room with the most dangerous artifacts. Unfortunately, greed corrupts like nothing else. Not many of us, human or magical, are immune to it."

He nodded. "I'll see you tomorrow then."

"Bye."

As he left, I turned to Sebille. "Stay close. Just in case."

Without a word, Sebille shifted into her Sprite form and flew skyward, hovering overhead.

With the comforting sound of her buzzing overhead, I moved over and sat down on the roof near Birte.

21

BEWARE THE ICE CREAM SIGN

"*A*re you all right?"

Birte sniffed and glowered at me from under her lashes. "Just peachy."

I didn't blame her for being mad. Her whole world had been uprooted. "The black dragon...that was your sister?"

She frowned. "Penny."

"Penny from Enchanted Collateral?" I already knew the answer from glimpsing Penny's tiny form on the roof, but I wanted Birte to verify it.

Birte took a deep, shuddering breath and scraped tears off her cheeks with the back of her hand. "She's the smart one. The good one. The one who went to college to get a degree in economics. But what did she do with it?" Birte's gaze shot to mine, anger roiling the flames that never seemed far from the surface. But she blinked and the fire receded, leaving behind only the sad blue gaze she showed the world. "She let her greed get the best of her and ended up in this stupid place, peddling dreams to people who wouldn't recognize true happiness if it bit them in the wing."

"She was making money off the artifact?"

Birte nodded. "Some guy brought it to her one day and offered to give her a cut if she'd launder the gold coins for his relative. Every time the relative used the artifact, he gave Penny half of what he created and she gave half of that to the guy."

"Can you tell me what the guy looked like?" I asked.

She described Fu Yen without hesitation. At least I was happy we'd found and dealt with the source of the problem in the PTB. "Did the money poison Penny?" I asked, looking for a way to help the young girl escape a lifetime behind bars at Area 51. Maybe I could make sure she served her time at a medical facility instead. Artifact poisoning was a recognized disease in the magical universe.

"Yes, and no. It definitely made her worse. But Penny's always been a bit on the greedy side." Birte shrugged. "I don't care that much about stuff, which is why I live up here. I enjoy my nest under the sky. It's peaceful and soothing."

I followed her unhappy gaze around the roof. Her nest had been destroyed. "I'm so sorry about this."

She stared at her hands. "It's my fault. I should have turned Penny in sooner. She was out of control. But when she killed Gus..."

"The man in the alley?" I asked.

"Yes. He was my friend. Just a human guy. Homeless. But he was kind to me."

And I was guessing a shy, plain-looking woman with a chip on her shoulder like Birte probably didn't find a lot of kindness in the world. "Why'd she kill him?" I asked.

"He'd picked up a coin she dropped." Birte frowned "I'm sure he was just going to give it back to her, but after killing that restaurant owner so she could keep all the gold for herself, she'd gotten very possessive about the gold. I didn't even recognize her anymore."

"You were going to tell the police?"

"Yes. I took one of the coins and planted it on Gus so you'd make the connection. Then I hid the artifact from Penny until I could get rid of it." Birte lifted her gaze, her expression earnest. "I was going to bring it to you."

I reached out and touched her hand, giving it a squeeze. I felt the instinctual rejection of my touch, but she bit the inside of her lip and didn't pull away. After a moment, she squeezed my hand back. "I'm sorry I didn't tell you the truth the first time."

I nodded. "Family is hard," I said.

Birte shrugged. "Penny isn't technically my

family. We just call each other sisters because there are no other dragons around." She frowned. "She's got something else magical in her that makes her stronger than I am."

I was pretty sure I knew what that was. Penny had told us she was half Elf. I'd assumed the other half was human, but I'd been wrong. "Will you be all right?"

"She'll be fine," a gravelly voice behind me said.

Birte and I turned to find Theo standing in the doorway to the vestibule. He gave me a guilty look, his cheeks pink. "I apologize, Naida keeper. I shouldn't have lied about the girls."

I was less inclined to forgive *him* than I was Birte. Theo and I had been friends for a couple of years. I'd believed we were beyond that kind of treatment. "You endangered everyone," I told him. "And Birte's lost her nest."

He pressed his lips together. "I know. And I'll help her rebuild it." He looked at Birte. "You can take anything you want from the shop. As much as you need. We'll rebuild your home together."

Fresh tears slipped down her cheeks, and I gave in to the impulse to pull her into a hug. "I'll see what I can do about getting Penny put into a hospital instead of prison. You'll be able to visit her as much as you want."

She took another shuddering breath. "Thank you so much, Naida keeper."

I looked her in the eye. "It's nothing. What are friends for?"

She gave me a watery smile and chuckled softly, shaking her head.

I stood up and headed for the vestibule, Sebille buzzing along behind me. At the door, I stopped and looked up at Theo. "You and I will have some work to do to repair this."

He nodded. "I know. I'm really sorry, Naida."

I stared at him a moment longer and then reached out and squeezed his forearm. It felt like rock beneath my fingers. "Be good to her. You owe her that."

His glance toward Birte was filled with more than affection. I thought there might have even been a little love in there.

Would wonders never cease? A giant and a dragon in love. The world was truly filled with miracles.

"Come on, Sprite. I'm starving."

Sebille landed full-sized on the roof behind me. All I had to do was mention food, and my assistant would fling her true form to the wind to join the tasty fun. "You wouldn't be starving if you hadn't blown off the beautiful dinner I cooked for you."

"Don't start with me," I told her as I bounced down the steps. "I was kind of busy."

"I cooked my fingers to the bone..."

"Stop it right now, Sebille. This is creepy. We're not married, you know."

"I'm just asking for a little consideration. When you're going to be late, a simple phone call is all that's necessary."

"You're being a total derf. You know that, right?" I shoved the ground floor door open and emerged into less smoky air. Across the street, Berbie honked and his doors flew open in greeting.

Sebille clacked along next to me in her ugly red shoes, a smile on her freckled face. "Fortunately, I know how you can make it up to me."

I stopped at the car, giving her a look. "I can't wait to hear this. How can I make it up to you, Sebille?"

She slipped inside. "You can get me ice cream."

I rolled my eyes. "Tadpole trampolines! You too?" I headed around Berbie and slipped behind the wheel. "Was there a sidekick convention tonight and you all decided to buy stock in ice cream shops?"

She snorted. "Sidekick convention, har de har, Naida. I want peanut butter fudge ripple with whipped cream on top. And you're paying."

I sighed. "Berbie..."

The little car shot away from the curb, no doubt heading for the nearest ice cream shop.

When had I totally lost control of my life?

"Okay, but if we run into the witch and the raven you're sleeping in Berbie tonight."

Berbie tooted his horn and took a turn on one wheel. The Dairy Freeze loomed up ahead, all bright lights and giant ice cream cone signs.

I grinned, suddenly realizing I could use an ice cream myself. That sign was oddly compelling.

Oh no! What if it was an artifact? I nearly groaned. I'd had more than my fill of artifacts for the night.

I'd deal with the ice cream compelling road sign another day. For the moment, there was a brownie chunk French vanilla sundae with hot fudge calling my name.

And I was totally planning on answering.

The End

READ MORE ENCHANTING INQUIRIES

Did you enjoy Fortune Croakies? If so, you might want to check out Book 3 of Enchanting Inquiries.

Please enjoy Chapter One of Gram Croakies, my gift to you!

Beauty isn't only fleeting, it can actually be deadly!

My favorite customer, Mrs. Foxladle, finds herself at odds with her book club friends over a curious obsession with youth and beauty. While the disagreement seems to have saved the octogenarian from being returned to the earliest moments of her existence...literally...it isn't doing anything to keep her from looking guilty for the deaths of her friends. There's no doubt in my mind I'm dealing with a rogue magical artifact in the hands of someone with diabolical intent. Unfortunately, I have no idea how to find either the artifact or the person wielding it.

It will be up to me and Detective Grym to find the culprits. Except that, Grym's timetable might just be a bit on the wonky side too. Which leaves solving the mystery up to me and my friends.

It's just a really good thing I have a cat and a frog and... Yeah, about that... I'm really no closer to figuring out how to use *them* either. Troll boogers! This magic wrangling stuff is hard!

GRAM CROAKIES

I was sipping a cup of tea and going over my notes from the last artifact I'd wrangled when the bell on the door to Croakies jangled. My cat, Mr. Wicked trotted from the back of the bookstore and jumped up onto the counter in front of me, his orange gaze fixed on the man who'd just entered Croakies.

Detective Wise Grym stood just inside the door, a large metal box clutched in his hands and rain dripping from his dark hair.

"Ribbit!" Mr. Slimy said from his place inside the glass fish tank I'd placed on a table near the counter. He hopped over a shiny collection of smooth rocks and flung himself against the glass as if he wanted to welcome the detective himself.

Or give him warts.

Given the fact that the frog was still serving as a squishy green bus for one arrogant witch with trust issues where law enforcement was concerned, it could easily be the latter.

As if reading my thoughts, a misty, semi-transparent haze rose from the frog and settled onto the carpet, depositing a ghost witch alongside the fish tank. "What's gargoyle man doing here?" Rustin asked snottily.

I fought a roll of my eyes at the demeaning reference to Grym's magical form. I wasn't supposed to tell anybody I'd found out what he was, but since nobody but me, Wicked and Sebille could see or hear the ghost witch, I'd felt like it was okay to tell him.

Sebille already knew anyway, she'd been there on that rooftop with me when the gargoyle had taken on the dragon whose miniaturized form had once filled the box in his hands.

"Detective Grym. You finally brought my box back." A week late.

Grym took one look at my red-rimmed eyes and frowned. "Are you sick?"

I barely kept from grimacing. I was sick all right. Sick of trying to co-exist with a noisy, messy, bossy Sprite whose promised "temporary" habitation in my beloved private space was going on ten days, three hours, forty-one minutes and twenty-three seconds. Make that twenty-four seconds.

Twenty-five...

I couldn't sleep because of Sebille's whistling

snores, and I hadn't gotten to watch my favorite television shows more than a handful of times since
she'd moved in with me. I'm not even going to
mention the ridiculous, claustrophobic chaos of
having all her furniture stuffed into my small place
alongside mine. Okay, I mentioned it, but it's not my
fault. The mess was making me cray!

The worst part of it all was that Sebille didn't
seem to care a whit about looking for a new place to
live. She seemed perfectly happy cooking her foul-
smelling concoctions on my stove and snoring on
her couch in my living room. The only peace I ever
seemed to get anymore was when the bossy Sprite
went next door to visit with her mother, the Queen
of the Fae, who was living in my friend Lea's greenhouse in the lot behind of our two shops.

I dropped my pen and came around the short
counter, moving toward the handsome detective
with a finger against my lips.

His frown deepened.

"Hello, Detective. How are you?"

He shook his head, not understanding my
warning to silence.

"You've outdone yourself this time, hon," Mrs.
Foxladle said, coming around the end of the
shelving for the mystery aisle with four paperbacks
piled in her arms. "I want to thank you for pointing
me toward the *Bewildered Basset Mysteries*. I find I
quite enjoy them, despite the fact that the cat has

second billing to the hound..." She jerked to a stop when she laid eyes on the Detective, a sly grin curving her lips. "Well, hello there, young man."

Grym shuffled from foot to foot under the older woman's assessing gaze. But I think it was probably the wink she threw me, as if Grym and I were an item, that discombobulated him the most.

"Mrs. Foxladle, this is Detective Grym," I told her. "He's the one who told me about the Basset Mysteries." I threw him a bright smile. "Aren't you, Detective?"

Of course that was a lie, dang lie and his quick glare was almost more fun than my anticipation of his response.

"Um. Yes. I...erm...love those books."

Mrs. Foxladle leaned a square hip against the shelves, a gleam in her eyes. "How fun! Which one do you like best, Detective? I'll read that one next."

My smile widened as I anticipated the verbal calisthenics Grym would need to employ to get out of answering her question.

But he surprised me by looking as if he were actually considering the query. "That's a really hard question for me," he told Mrs. Foxladle."

I almost laughed. I just bet it was.

"Book one was predictably the weakest story, plot-wise, but I have to say I loved the characters so much in that one. I particularly thought Basil was charming. And Penelope was irresistible. Book two,

Befuddled Basil Baulks, had a much better story but I thought the author lost a bit of her love of Basil and Pene's relationship in the mix."

I felt my mouth falling open but was helpless to stop it, despite the smug glance the detective sent my way.

Before he even completed his astounding assertion, Mrs. Foxladle's gaze had lost its teasing glint and she was nodding with excitement. "My thoughts exactly," she told him, tugging a book out of the pile. "Have you read the third book yet?"

Grym nodded, pointing to the title. "I think you'll be pleasantly surprised. The author managed to meld the best aspects of the first two books and came up with a really strong mystery premise in three."

Mrs. Foxladle jittered happily, her eyes sparkling with pleasure. "It's so much fun to meet another mystery connoisseur, she told him happily. "I wonder," The elderly book lover reached into her purse and pulled out a small, white rectangle, handing it to Grym. "Would you like to join our Book Club, Detective? It would be ever so much fun discussing the mysteries with a real, live police detective."

He paled, his gaze spinning to mine, filled with panic. "Um..."

I decided I'd teased him enough. "Why don't we get you checked out, Mrs. Foxladle," I told my favorite customer. "I'm sure Detective Grym needs to get back to work."

"Of course." She patted his hand. "I'm so sorry to have kept you." But before she followed me across to the register, she tucked the card into the pocket of his jacket, winking coyly. "I hope you'll join us, Detective."

He gave her a smile, nodding. "Thanks for the invitation. It's very kind."

Grym disappeared between the bookshelves as I was checking out Mrs. Foxladle and I thought he was probably hiding among the reference books hoping to avoid more pressure from the kindly old woman. But her comment about book club reminded me. "It's Tuesday. Aren't you supposed to be at book club tonight?" I asked as I handed over her purchases.

Wicked rubbed against her arm as she took it, purring loudly as she scratched between his dark gray ears.

Mrs. Foxladle's lip curled slightly at my question. "I decided to skip this week, hon. I didn't care for the book we were discussing at all."

"Oh, that's too bad. I know how much you enjoy those meetings."

She shrugged, her expression darkening for just a moment before she forced a smile onto her face. "I wish everyone was as conscious of my feelings as you are, Naida." She patted my hand and turned away, her steps not quite as lively as usual.

I watched her go, feeling as if there was something wrong in her world and wishing I could fix it. "Goodnight, Mrs. Foxladle."

"Goodnight, hon." She lifted her head, gaze focused on the shelves of books running the depth of the store. "Goodbye, Detective."

She didn't wait for him to respond, which was a good thing because Grym didn't emerge from the stacks for a couple of minutes. And when he did, his expression wasn't happy.

I noticed that the card she'd given him was clutched in his hand. "What's wrong?" I asked, coming out from behind the counter.

His gaze slid to me, worry darkening the melted caramel color to dull brown.

I pointed to the card. "Are you considering joining the book club?" I grinned to show him I was teasing, but he didn't grin back.

Ice formed on my spine. "What's wrong, Grym?"

He lifted the card, showing it to me. "This address..."

I tried to see the address on the card but his fingers obscured the text on the front. "What about it?"

The detective looked at the card again, shifting his fingers so he could read the information typed on its surface. He shook his head, swallowing before answering. "It's why I came here tonight. There's been a magical incident." He lifted his focus from the card, his gaze haunted. "Five ladies. The landlord told me they had book club every Tuesday evening."

The ice spread until my lungs were frozen and I had trouble taking a deep breath. My hand was suddenly covering my face. "An artifact?"

"It has to be," he told me. "Nothing else could have done what..." He swallowed hard again as his gaze slid to the door. "Her friends are all..."

I made a soft sound, turning my gaze toward the door again. "Poor Mrs. Foxladle," I murmured.

Grym nodded, finally seeming to shake off his horror, his gaze tightening as it settled on me. "Will you come to the scene with me? I'd really like your opinion. And if the artifact is still in the apartment..."

I nodded. "Of course. Let me just tell Sebille I'm stepping out."

There were no bodies in the room.

In fact, to my eye, there wasn't really much at all to point to murder or even natural death. I stood back as Grym examined the floor around the table closely and then bent with a magnifying glass to scrutinize the seat of each chair in turn.

Watching from a couple of feet away, I squinted

at the spot where he was looking and saw nothing. Except maybe a tiny spot in the center of the chair, which just looked like a food crumb to me.

I cast my gaze around the place, noting the abundance of upholstered furniture covered in chintz fabric and glossy wood tables protected by what looked like homemade doilies.

The room smelled like a combination of lemon dusting spray and the sweet scent of lilacs from an overflowing vase filled with fresh flowers at a nearby table.

The table Grym was perusing appeared to be an inexpensive rectangular folding table, covered in a flowery tablecloth that hung nearly to the floor on the long sides. Six metal folding chairs were arranged around it, only one of them still pushed up under the table.

I blinked rapidly as I realized that had to be Mrs. Foxladle's place. It was a miracle she'd decided not to attend the club meeting that night. As far as I knew, she rarely missed her meetings.

I checked out the surface of the table, seeing a teacup filled with varying levels of cold tea at each place. The cups were painted with pastel flowers and each one had a tiny bee painted into the inside, looking as if it was climbing toward the lip. They were adorable.

"It doesn't look like they had time to drink their tea," I offered helpfully.

Each place setting also sported a well-worn paperback. I smiled sadly when I recognized the bookmarks I'd had done with depictions of Mr. Wicked and Mr. Slimy inside a couple of them.

A plate that looked as if it had been loaded up with baked goods was empty, except for one small muffin and some crumbs. I wondered if the muffins had been poisoned.

Each setting had a small plate nearby, more crumbs attesting to the fact that the ladies had enjoyed a nice snack before they...

I swallowed hard.

Next to one plate was a grease spot that probably came from an unwrapped muffin or maybe a cookie. That particular plate had no crumbs, as if the person sitting there had either foregone the snack or had dropped the muffin onto the tablecloth instead, creating the grease spot.

If the ladies who'd been in that room really did turn up dead or missing, I didn't envy Grym's job trying to figure out what had happened. "Are you sure the women didn't just leave?" I asked Grym. "Who reported the m missing?"

Grym straightened, his expression tight. "They didn't leave." He scanned a glance around the room.

"But then where are their bodies?"

Instead of answering me, he frowned more deeply.

"Detective?"

He shook his head and moved to the table, using the magnifying glass on the items scattered across the top while ignoring my questions.

"I can't help if you won't talk to me."

He continued to ignore me, his focus locked on his search.

I sighed. Stepping back from the table, I tugged my keeper magic forward and lifted my hands, sending it into the air and watching as several thin gray ribbons of magic wove away from my fingers and slithered throughout the apartment, disappearing from sight.

There were no chimes of discovery.

One strand headed for the table and wound around the remaining muffin before sliding across the table, hesitating on the grease spot, and then wrapping around Grym's arm like a bracelet.

He lifted a scowl in my direction.

"Oops! Sorry," I said, giving him an embarrassed smile. "Just trying to help."

He straightened, shaking his arm to dispel the ribbon of magic. It dissipated with a soft hiss as he headed in my direction. "Don't touch anything."

I frowned. "I haven't touched anything..."

He handed me the magnifying glass. "The seats of the chairs."

Grym stared at me for a moment as I realized he was answering my questions. "Ah. Show, don't tell," I said, nodding. "Got it."

I moved to the closest chair and leaned over it, focusing the magnifying glass over the seat as he'd done, and saw... "Nothing."

He frowned, taking the glass from my hand and giving the seat a long examination. "Hm," he said. His glance skimmed to the paperback, teacup, and empty plate at that spot.

The detective moved to the next chair, looking up after just a moment. "This one."

I took the glass again and bent over the seat, focusing it on the tiny speck I saw at the very center of the vinyl.

The "spot" was actually comprised of two things, a tiny, lima-bean-shaped clump of something lying in a pool of liquid. I moved the magnifying glass closer and squinted at the teeny, tiny...

I jumped back with a yelp, dropping the glass as I stumbled backward, putting as much distance as I could between me and the object on that chair. My horrified gaze lifted to Grym's finding its match on his face. "Holy alligator pajamas."

He nodded. "Do you see why I believe it's a magical artifact?"

I nodded, my gaze sliding back to the chair as dizziness swamped me. My heart was pounding so hard in my chest I thought I might pass out. "Please tell me that wasn't what I thought it was."

"I wish I could, Naida keeper." He scrubbed a big hand over his bristly jaw, sending the scratchy sound of whiskers against skin into the painfully silent room. "But I'm pretty sure that, whatever killed those women, did it by returning them to their youngest possible forms."

"The ultimate anti-aging product," I murmured in revulsion, as my heart tried to bang its way through my ribs.

———

Check out the entire series here: https://samcheever. com/books/#enchanting

ALSO BY SAM CHEEVER

If you enjoyed **Fortune Croakies**, you might also enjoy these other fun mystery series by Sam. To find out more, visit the **BOOKS** page at www. samcheever.com:

Reluctant Familiar Paranormal Mysteries
Yesterday's Paranormal Mysteries
Gainfully Employed Mysteries
Silver Hills Cozy Mysteries
Country Cousin Mysteries

ABOUT THE AUTHOR

USA Today and WSJ Bestselling Author Sam Cheever writes contemporary and paranormal mystery and suspense, creating stories that draw you in and keep you eagerly turning pages. Known for writing great characters, snappy dialogue, and unique and exhilarating stories, Sam is the award-winning author of 80+ books.

To learn more about Sam and her work, visit her at one of her online hotspots:
www.samcheever.com
samcheever@samcheever.com

Made in the USA
Middletown, DE
20 September 2019